ON THE SEVENTH DAY

ALSO BY T.D. JAKES

ON THE SEVENTH DAY

A NOVEL

T.D. JAKES

ATRIA BOOKS

NEW YORK   LONDON   TORONTO   SYDNEY   NEW DELHI

ATRIA BOOKS
A Division of Simon & Schuster, Inc.
1230 Avenue of the Americas
New York, NY 10020

First Atria Books hardcover edition October 2012

ATRIA BOOKS and colophon are trademarks of Simon & Schuster, Inc.

For information about special discounts for bulk purchases, please contact Simon & Schuster Special Sales at 1-866-506-1949 or business@simonandschuster.com.

The Simon & Schuster Speakers Bureau can bring authors to your live event. For more information or to book an event, contact the Simon & Schuster Speakers Bureau at 1-866-248-3049 or visit our website at www.simonspeakers.com.

Designed by Akasha Archer

Manufactured in the United States of America

10 9 8 7 6 5 4 3 2 1

Library of Congress Cataloging-in-Publication Data
Jakes, T.D.
  On the seventh day : a novel / T.D. Jakes. — 1st Atria Books hardcover ed.
  p. cm.
  1. Married people—Fiction. 2. Missing children—Fiction 3. New Orleans (La.)—Fiction. I. Title.
PS3610.A39O5 2012
813 '.6—dc23   2012022733
ISBN: 978–1–4391–7050–2
ISBN: 978–1–4391–7056–4 (ebook)

I would like to dedicate this novel to the women who have made immeasurable contributions to my life. My wife, Serita; my beloved late mother, Mrs. Odith P. Jakes; my sister, Jacqueline Jakes; my spiritual mother, Pastor Christine McCaskill; and my daughters, Cora Coleman and Sarah Henson. Each of these women has profoundly affected my life in significant ways. You all have been the wind beneath my wings.

It is said that God created the world in six days.
But there was no light . . .
No heaven and earth . . .
No creatures . . .
Except the beasts imagined in my mind.
And there was no me.
In those six days, I ceased to exist.

DARKNESS

— 1 —

David Ames could make a woman forget herself.

Kari knows because it just happened a few minutes ago on this quiet Sunday morning. Surrounded now by the hot water and steam of the shower, she reflects on the last hour and the intimate moments with her husband.

It feels good to forget. To just let go. Yet lately, it seems Kari hasn't been letting go as much as she'd like. Perhaps this is just what happens when a couple has been married for eight years. The thrill of a touch or a kiss is too often overshadowed by the needs of a child or the demands of a job.

With her eyes closed, Kari knows it's more than that. It will always be more than that.

The busy day ahead of her is put on pause as she thinks for a moment about David and wonders what got into him. They haven't made love like that for a while. She feels full but also curious, wondering what had triggered the sudden urge in him.

She can't remember the last time they had been intimate. Perhaps that's what caused it, the ticking clock of the calendar. Or maybe it came from the stress of David's job at Tulane University and the need to let it go. She doesn't know and didn't ask him afterward. She wants to enjoy this feeling and let everything else slip away.

The bathroom is a blanket of fog when she gets out of the shower and wraps a towel around herself. She can't help thinking of those days when she first encountered David, when a young and naive woman fell in love with his sensitivity and his smile. The well-dressed professor had always been very careful, never crossing the line or being inappropriate with her while she was in his class. David himself had only been teaching for a couple of years, yet he had still carried himself like a seasoned professional.

Professional or not, Kari knew the moment she stepped foot in his classroom what was on Professor Ames's mind. She knew more than most women what men really thought about, what really drove them.

Am I still the young woman he fell madly in love with? Kari wonders as she wipes a hand towel over the mirror to look at herself.

Inspecting herself in a mirror has never been a desirable thing, but she still likes what she sees looking back at her. Maybe she is thirty-six years old and maybe she's no longer the young woman in Professor Ames's classroom. There will always be someone younger and more attractive in his lecture hall. But there won't be another Kari.

David resisted at first, yet soon fell for her because she was strong. He told her that the first time they kissed in front of his old house. She fell for him because he was a gentleman, a man of faith who tried to live by that faith and not by a belief in himself.

Kari knows it's nice to be reminded how beautiful David thinks she is, and how well they fit one another. Physically and mentally.

It was a nice way to start the day. Yet as the steam fogs up the mirror again, Kari knows there are some things you can't escape.

Things like the past and the person you once were.

− 2 −

David Ames turns off the water and then opens the shower curtain. For a moment, he admires Kari from where he's standing. Soon any thought of time and getting ready dissolves as he finds a towel and then climbs out of the shower.

David can't help himself, moving behind Kari to wrap his arms around her. She looks like an angel in a silk slip standing in their steam-filled bathroom. She was wiping condensation from the mirror to reveal a vision of beauty that he wasn't even sure she herself was aware of. Something about seeing her, standing there: hair still damp, face so natural and new, makes him want her on this Sunday morning.

Again.

"You feel good," he tells her. She smiles toward the mirror.

"Uh huh," she says as she begins to moisturize her face. "And you're still wet."

He smiles, resisting the temptation to play with her words, to take the image further.

Marriage and becoming a mother haven't changed Kari much, David thinks. She's still sexy and still stubborn and she makes a wonderful mother to Mikayla. As he moves in behind her, he knows they fit like a glove and always have. Their humor, their similar interests in movies and music, the way both of them can be at peace not saying anything—Kari complements him in the same way he does her.

"Remember when you weren't so busy to get ready for the day?" David teases.

"Remember when we didn't have so many things going on in

our lives?" she replies as she smiles at his errant hand. "It's hard trying
to accommodate all your friends."

"All of *my* friends? They're our friends now."

"I know. But they all bring expectations, especially when they're
coming over later in the day."

"It's gonna be a glorious day, I just know it," David says as he rubs
his palms against her soft skin.

Yes indeed, some things in life just fit, and David and Kari are one
of them. They are regular churchgoers, but nonetheless, his passion
for her could make everything—church, breakfast, their daughter—
evaporate in a single moment of longing.

"Let's go back to bed," he whispers in her ear. "I can take you
there. . . ."

She slowly and gently moves his hands, turning to face him. "I
need to get ready—and so do you."

There's something about Kari that makes the normally conser-
vative and serious man want to be different. He has often joked that
she makes him wilder, while Kari has said he has made her more
structured and disciplined. This contrast has made their relationship
work.

He looks down at those eyes of hers. It's easy to get lost in them
and lose sight of life's other responsibilities. She's always been able to
take him far away whenever it's just been the two of them.

"It won't take me long to get ready," he says, his hands still on her,
still refusing to let go.

Kari smiles, both in humor and in affection. But as she eases her
body away, David knows it's a losing battle. She's already in her busy
mode, in her zone of mommy and wife and woman duties. After one
last kiss on her neck, he heads back into the bedroom, burying his
feelings inside for later. He is surprised to find a suit, shirt, and bow tie
waiting for him on the chair. She must have laid it out moments ago
when he was in the shower. He quickly puts on the pants and shirt.

"Like the new tie?"

He looks at the bathroom doorway to see her smiling. "Woman, is there anything you can't do?"

"I don't know. Can't think of anything. You hungry?"

"Starved. But I know you don't wanna be late for church so I'll wait."

Kari gives him a knowing look. "Breakfast is downstairs on the table. We have time for that."

My lady knows how to treat me right, he thinks.

"When did you have time to cook?"

Kari moves over with her back to him, inviting him to zip up her dress. "Today's the cake sale, remember. I've been up since six. Those deacons are vicious about their cakes."

"You're really not making this easy on me, are you," he says, focused on her smooth, sleek skin.

"Just keep zipping."

Just as he's about to tell her how good she looks, the tall, four-year-old bolt of energy comes running into the room holding two dresses.

"Which one should I wear, Daddy?" Mikayla asks. "Yellow or purple?"

The young girl is tall and slender like her mother, and looks more like six than her age. "I like the yellow, but ask your mother."

"Well, I ironed the purple," Kari says. "Mommy loves purple because it's the color of hope, it's magical."

"I love magic, Mommy," she shouts, running to give Mommy a big hug.

"Then purple it is, my little princess."

David knows that women have a mind of their own, whether they're almost forty or only four years old. *Never mind what Daddy likes,* David thinks. He knows he's already outnumbered by these two strong, beautiful women.

"C'mon, let's get some breakfast so Mommy can finish dressing." David sees Kari's smile as he takes Mikayla's hand.

— 3 —

He watches and waits, hungry for something he can't have, but eventually will. Behind the wheel of a nondescript, plain, gray van, the driver ignores the familiar New Orleans scenery, the scars of Katrina, the Creole cottages, and shotgun houses. Crossing the Mississippi River, he holds his breath.

His mind conjures images and thoughts and actions that others would fear and be repulsed by. Wanting. Everlasting want.

His body shivers for a moment as he finally lets out the breath slowly.

Nobody knows his name, nor pays him any attention—and that's just fine.

He's passing pristine houses in an unpolluted world where he doesn't belong. Victorian and Greek Revival homes that look to be out of the pages of some magazine. The white pillars of the mansions seem to stand guard in rigid fashion, watching him as he drives by. They usually ward off strangers, but not today, not him.

He stops, having found what he's after.

Pretty little faces. Smiling. Laughing. Playing.

At a corner intersection, he slows down at a stop sign. Watching. Unblinking. Unwavering.

His heart and his breathing are steady and deliberate. Just like everything else he does. Clean and orderly and steady and silent.

He stirs up stacks of candy bars, lollypops, and small toys with his right hand. Puts just a few in his pocket as he looks for a place to park. Plenty of children take the candy, and plenty of parents forget to watch them. And he knows more than anybody that it only takes five seconds for everything to change and for this pink-and-purple world to turn black.

One girl looks his direction and then looks away quickly. Another sees the van and then looks around for her mommy.

But another with little pigtails studies the van, smiling.

The driver keeps slowly moving, watching, waiting.

— 4 —

The sun beams brightly, even through Kari's sunglasses, as she climbs out of the car and watches David begin to guide Mikayla toward church. She loves seeing their relationship, knowing not every daughter in this world has a caring father like David. For a second she presses down the new dress, trying to wipe away the wrinkles made by the seat belt. She walks around to remove a cake from the trunk, hoping that the morning humidity hasn't begun to melt the frosting. A plain-dressed woman in the parking lot catches her attention. She's holding flyers of some kind in her hand.

A familiar face walks up to greet her. "Am I gonna be able to try a piece of that?"

Kari smiles at Tia, one of her closest friends. "You better be fast."

They're still by the car when the woman with the flyers walks up to them. Tia takes one and they both glance at the image. The smiling face of a young girl is pictured on it and large type reads, "If You See this Child . . ."

"Aren't you in the wrong neighborhood?" Tia asks. "The abductions were on the other side of the river."

The woman—her skin cracked and blemished, her eyes cold—speaks with a deep accent. "West Bank, East Bank . . . the way I see it, bad people are everywhere."

Next to Kari and Tia, who are both wearing their Sunday best, this woman looks out of place. She nods at them and then slinks away.

Kari wants to catch up to her and tell her that she understands, to tell her that not everybody in this neighborhood is as quick to judge as her outspoken friend, yet she doesn't. Another part of her is afraid of exposing something she buried long ago, someone she would rather forget about.

She uses the cake as an excuse not to act, knowing it needs to get inside soon or it will be a soupy mess.

Tia shakes her head. "I read in the *Times-Picayune* all those little girls came from single-mother homes. Maybe if those women had been watching their children instead of hanging in the streets, their kids wouldn't have been snatched up by some psycho."

"Tia, that's not fair. Stop being so judgmental."

Tia gives her the flyer. "Girl, you know it's the truth."

If only you knew the truth, Kari thinks.

Deep down, Tia has a good heart. She's just lived a sheltered life with a set of stable parents who both stuck around her whole life.

Not everybody has it so easy. Not everybody gets to grow up and marry a doctor and live happily ever after.

Kari knows those streets well. She knows that not everybody walking them is doing so by choice. Some people aren't handed the present of a future when they're young. Some have to figure out how to make it on their own.

A figure rushing and out of breath walks up beside Tia. Les, her husband, grabs her hand. "Good morning, Kari," he says. "C'mon, honey."

Les, the doctor, is always busy, always rushing. Kari notices the large man's body language as he guides his wife in to church the same way David was guiding Mikayla.

Men always gotta be showin' us the way, in one way or another, Kari thinks.

She looks more closely at the picture on the flyer, but in a second heads into church. The cake she's holding is getting heavy. But more than that, she doesn't want to think of the evil that's out there.

As she heads toward the church, she spots Mikayla running

around with a couple of friends, considers the flyer of the missing child, and thanks God that she knows where her daughter is.

"Time to go inside, Mikayla."

The four-year-old is animated, but seems fulfilled for the moment. She gives one of her friends a high five and then joins her parents as they head toward the opened doors of the church.

− 5 −

A stone's throw from those very same doors, eyes stay fixed on a single, solitary soul.

The creamy dark skin, the white smile, the bright eyes, the laugh and life that stand out.

She smiles and laughs and plays and doesn't have the slightest idea what's hiding so close to her. He smiles to himself.

Under the shadows of a large oak tree draped in Spanish moss, the parked van is silent and so is he. He watches the children in front of the church from across the street. Their parents are close by and not a bit worried or wondering about their children.

The little girl who joins her parents and holds their hands as they go into sanctuary is the one.

She's a charming little postcard that needs to be taken and tacked on a bulletin board.

A charming little smile that needs to be admired by one and only one.

— 6 —

The congregation is packed as usual, a multiethnic group that loves to sing and worship. There is genuine joy in these pews, a spirit flowing through them that makes this place feel more like home than church. David finds his usual seat near his friends and Mikayla takes her seat on his lap. Soon they're watching the choir come in and searching for Mommy.

As the sweet sound of "Someone Watching Over Me" sweeps over them, David sees Mikayla waving.

"Hi, Mommy," she says, loud enough for everyone around her to hear.

Kari smiles and waves back as she continues to sing the uplifting song. Hearing it puts David's soul at peace. This is the place he needs to be, with the women God has blessed him with.

Les and Tia are sitting in front of him, and David can see Les typing something away on his phone as he ignores the singing. David has known Les ever since they were roommates at Tulane. That was probably the only way they would have ever come across each other and become friends. Les is one of the few people David knows who is busier than him.

David knows it's good to leave work behind, especially in this place on this day.

Sometimes the week can't be over too soon for this final day of rest to wash over him. It fills his soul. Fills and renews his soul, readying him for another busy week, which only takes and drains.

"This seat taken?" a woman's voice asks out of the blue.

David looks and sees a gaunt, pale face and dull eyes staring at him. He doesn't need to wonder what her story is except for the fact that she's standing next to his pew asking to sit down.

"All yours," he says.

David feigns a smile, but feels uncomfortable and a bit awkward as he moves and lets the woman sit down next to him. The clothes that don't fit her and that lost gaze give her away. She's more suited for the city streets far from here than for the comfortable pews.

Bishop T.D. Jakes takes the pulpit and David's attention is taken away from her.

"Hope y'all feel rested this morning 'cause it's the seventh day!"

The grin on David's face, which isn't going away anytime soon, is real and genuine. Mikayla is still in his lap, watching and moving and most importantly, listening.

"Put your Bibles down and settle yourself," the bishop continues. "'Cause we about to get resurrected!"

The congregation is nodding and urging Bishop Jakes on, excited to take this journey with him, eager to see what God has in store for them.

— 7 —

It doesn't take long for the sweet sanctuary of the church to open its doors and give way to the Boys Club, which David is a part of.

Outside under the clear sky and hot sun, Les is in his too-tight suit next to Wayne in his too-expensive shades. The doctor and the lawyer standing side by side. David knows this could be the start of a joke. All of them are standing there listening to Arthur, who always talks a big game. This is the guys' post-benediction ritual as they wait for their ladies to leave church to go home.

"Man, we finally closed the deal, but it took an act of Congress to get those folks out of that project," Arthur says.

"What's gonna happen to all those people?" David asks.

"They got some cash and thirty days' notice. Most of 'em will go to East New Orleans—or find a rental somewhere. What's important is that I can finally knock that mess down and get this mall built. Katrina was good to some of us."

This comment didn't surprise David. He sometimes joked with Kari that the easygoing-yet-slick Arthur was his bougie brother—out to sell the world and willing to give up his soul.

Two women walk by the posse of men, but only Beth gets noticed. She's the one in the high heels and the legs running a mile long—the shapely beauty that doesn't walk, but rather slides by like a skater on cool ice. A skater *knowing* she's being watched.

"Good morning, gentlemen," she says.

"Morning, Beth," David says to his assistant.

Beth Hutchins has worked for him for the past three years, yet it's only been the last six months since she began to attend his church. He met her the same way he met Kari, when she first began attending his class. The only difference was that David was married when he met Beth.

It didn't stop her until I had to put a stop to it.

David shoves the thought away as Beth gives him a brief but friendly glance. The men greet Beth and then follow her with their eyes as she walks away.

"Man, if you're not gonna hit that—I will," Arthur whispers to David.

David just shakes his head. "Arthur, sometimes I wonder about you. Didn't you *just* ask a woman to marry you?"

"Yeah, but a fine thing like that could make me change my mind."

David keeps quiet about Beth as a matter of respect for himself and for his wife and family. He's never been one to talk about women the way someone like Arthur does, treating them like objects rather than people. Yet David understands where his friend is coming from. He recognizes Beth's beauty too. It had been a point of contention with himself about hiring her. In the end, though, David hired her because of her mind and her work ethic, her ability to get the students' attention when necessary. A situation perfectly illustrated by the glances trailing after Beth. David is the only one to stop following her every movement.

He's learned better.

— 8 —

The women focus on Beth too. The women were busy chatting after church as usual before Beth came and stopped the conversation. Now they stand there watching the scene nearby.

"I wish I had her legs," Grace says.

"It looks like your man's wishing you had her legs too, the way he's staring," Pam says.

Kari is surprised to hear Pam say such a thing, but she knows that Pam tends to say and do things for effect.

"Legs or no legs, I don't like her," Tia says, brushing back her hair. "Every Sunday, she's here flaunting her stuff."

Kari notices all the men except David looking Beth's way. It's a good sign. They've talked about Beth before. Kari has shared her concern in the past about David working with such an attractive woman, but David has always assured her that he only views her as an assistant. Yet Kari still watches him whenever she's around. Just to be careful.

As Beth climbs into her car, the men give her a wave.

"Girl, I'm not even worried about that," Grace says, taking the perfect opportunity to share her good news. "I got my ring!"

The girls all stop and gather around her with excitement and loud admiration, looking at diamonds that compete in brilliance with the sun. Everybody knows that Arthur wants nothing more than to have a trophy wife to show off to everybody. Kari knows that money can buy a lot, and it sure took a lot of it to buy that diamond ring.

"Kari, do you need me to bring anything to the barbecue?" Tia asks once the celebrating and grandstanding are over.

"No, I'm all set. Just bring yourself and these characters," Kari says, waving toward the guys.

Arthur is the first to greet them. He puts out his arms to Grace.

"There you are, baby. I've been looking all over for you."

Grace embraces him as if she actually believes him. The rest of the group just watch the two and laugh.

The golf ball has never been used before. After Les Walker tees it up and launches it with his driver, they all realize that the golf ball will never be used again. It is swallowed by the blue pond that lines the fairway at the English Turn Country Club.

"Are you sure you've played here before?" David asks his out-of-shape friend.

"If you'd bought here 'stead of the East Bank, you wouldn't have to slum balls at City Park," Les ribs David.

David squints and wipes sweat off his forehead. "Have you seen City Park lately? It's no slum. I need to get you over there on the basketball court so you can lose some of that chub."

"Don't hate," Les says. "This chub comes from good living."

Wayne steps past David, holding a Callaway driver that probably cost a few hundred bucks and was recommended by the latest issue of *Golf Digest*. The lawyer nods and grins as he sets to tee off.

"You gotta admit, we are living the American dream," Wayne says. "Driving nice rides, in beautiful houses, investing in the market. We have superfine women, bruh. Isn't this what our ancestors fought for?"

"Last time I heard Martin's and Malcolm's speeches, they weren't talking about cars and women," David snaps back. "I'm pretty sure they were fighting for freedom and equality, which obviously didn't mean shit when Katrina came along."

"C'mon, man, those folks were in the wrong place at the wrong time," Wayne responds, sounding like he knows the button David aimed to push was on him.

Joking about ladies or golf is one thing, but some things can't help but get under David's skin. "If my mom hadn't been in the *wrong* place, she might be here today. You need to step back a little."

"No disrespect about your mom, man. I'm just sayin'—you don't have to have a rat bitin' your ass to be relevant."

David nods, takes his driver, and steps in front of Arthur. "Well, I guess you're right about that."

The men laugh as David hits a nice shot, which lands in the middle of the fairway.

"So, Les, you still bangin' that li'l nurse in the hospital closet?" Wayne asks.

A loud roar of laughter spills over the golf course.

"What can I say?" Les asks. "She makes me feel young. Tia and I don't spark like that anymore."

"So why am I getting married?" Arthur jokes.

"Every man needs a good woman next to him," David says to restore a bit of order. "I know I'm lucky to have Kari. She's a good wife, an awesome mother, and—"

"A super freak?" Wayne says.

More laughter.

"Chill, man. Kari's my angel."

Wayne nods and smiles. "Everybody knows angels don't get freaky in the bedroom. What happens when you hunger for a little something more?"

"Things change—with children, work, life," David says.

"So tell me again, *why* am I getting married?" Arthur asks, a confused look on his face, which makes them break into laughter again.

"So you and your wife and kids can pretend to live happily ever after in this lovely gated community with the rest of us," Les says.

"Oh, yes, all safe and secure," David says with full sarcasm. "I don't know, man—this idea that I need to live behind gates so I can protect myself from the outside world is just paranoia."

Les gives him a smug glance with his round cheeks. "You do what you do, but I don't want to walk out of *my* house and find some beggar with his hand out."

"Really?" David responds as the other guys around him moan in unison. "Y'all can moan all you want, but what I want is to protect my family from high unemployment, the rising costs of health care, and jacked-up oil spills. Okay?"

Wayne smiles a million-dollar grin at him. "Some folks' worst nightmare is others folks' road to the American Dream. That's reality here in the land of capitalism. Isn't it?"

"You all are demented," David says.

"Say what you want. We're taking our demented butts straight to the bank!"

Arthur and Wayne give each other high fives and bumps on the shoulder as David gets in his golf cart followed by Les.

David is already tired of this conversation, and they have ten more holes to go. He knows they don't get it and maybe never will.

For a moment he thinks back on his youth, to growing up in Hollygrove in the seventeenth ward. It's a piece of him these other men don't know and will never know. He's not ashamed of where he came from, but he knows the box people put you in once they know where you've been in life.

This is one of the wonderful things about Kari, how she accepted him fully and how she even understood. She came from an estranged family he never had a chance to meet. He could tell she had been running for a long time from a youth she hated and from people she didn't want to be associated with.

Both of them met at a crossroads where they truly could live the American Dream. Freedom from the hopelessness of not having money and not being able to find work. Feeling the equality that they could succeed just like everybody else.

David enjoys these guys from his church and likes debating them about topics like this. They will never know why he feels this way, however. In their eyes, he's the professor.

If only they knew the truth. Not just about his broken past, but also about his spotted soul.

− 10 −

The stairs creak in the darkness with each step of the man's booted feet. The storage closet whines open.

A weak, lone bulb bathes the space in cold light.

Inside the empty closet go three things: a three-and-a-half-pound Porta Potti for a child, a case of twelve Hubig's pies in assorted flavors, and a pink stuffed kitty with a smile that doesn't belong in such a lonely place.

Kari is surveying everything in her mental to-do list now that the men have been back for several minutes from their golf outing.

David's got the crawfish boiling.

Check.

Wayne and Arthur are trying to show their manliness by standing by the grill.

Check.

She is carrying her homemade-to-perfection baked beans while Tia carries the potato salad and Pam carries the bread.

Check, check, check.

On the table outside, Kari makes sure everything else is in order.

"The world's not gonna end if everything isn't perfect," Tia tells her.

"You know I like things a certain way."

The kids are playing in the lawn and in the pool. The breeze outside is slight, making the cool drinks even more enjoyable and the cool pool tempting to even the grown-ups.

"Girl, I'm just glad you represent," Pam says. "There's nothing I wanna do in that kitchen except see someone else cook in it."

"Diva, I have a family. We don't live in restaurants like you and Wayne. Don't you know there's a recession going on?"

Pam looks over at Tia. "Personally, I think your soror's got issues."

"Or maybe she's just not gettin' any," Grace chimes in.

"Don't go there. I got enough to last me a lifetime," Kari says with a confident grin as she opens some napkins and then arranges the silverware.

"Well, Les and I are on the bimonthly plan, which suits me just fine," Tia says.

Grace walks over to Kari. "My mother says: a man in a bow tie is way too proper to treat a woman right."

"That big rock on your finger must have hit you over the head, talking like that. Guess your momma never met David. People aren't everything you see on the surface."

The ladies answer with a chorus of oohs and aahs just as the men join them.

"How was your game?" Pam asks as she sips a glass of white wine.

"The professor here shot forty-two," Wayne says, in the tone of a sore loser.

"I did it just to piss him off," David says with a laugh. "By the way, you owe me twenty bucks."

"Were you all betting again?" Tia asks.

"Gotta make it interesting," Les tells her.

David knows that Kari's wondering when he'll get to the grill and attend to the crawfish.

"Just a few more minutes," David says. "They're almost done."

"Thank you, honey. Folks are hungry."

He gives her a glance that reminds her of this morning.

Seems like the crawfish aren't the only things folks are hungry for around here.

Kari smiles back at David, wondering what's suddenly gotten in to him today, but not minding it one bit.

She hopes and prays that they won't ever lose it.

−12−

The Ames family's two-story house in the East Bank area sits in front of a beautiful wooded area, providing a picturesque privacy that also frames a yard bursting with life among friends.

Splashes from the pool, laughter, and grunts of badminton players provide their own kind of music. Kids run around as their parents mingle in and out of them. The afternoon is still vibrant and bright, but the woods are thick enough to block the sun and the view from the outside.

Boots at a near distance step over a branch and snap it in half, but the sound goes unheard.

Eyes watch closely, intently as one little girl swims in the shallow end of the pool, her arms and legs in pink and purple floaties. Her smile seems to keep her afloat.

Not far away from the girl is the father, next to a monster-size cauldron. Every few moments, he glances and talks to his girl to make sure she's okay and to keep her laughing. Soon he's gathering the crawfish and pouring them on the table.

The eyes watch, the figure hidden by a tree, unseen and undisturbed and completely undaunted.

−13−

The children eat quickly and then resume their fun in the pool. Soon David is sitting back with a full stomach, enjoying the rest of his beer. His wife is already starting to clean up and get ready for dessert.

"Baby, you've been in that pool all day," Kari calls out to their daughter.

"Just a little longer, Mommy."

As she starts to walk over to Mikayla, David gently taps her on her butt. She looks back and is reminded of the morning and her husband's failed effort to seduce her the second time. She's still busy doing mommy duty *and* cook duty *and* cleanup duty, but he's just sitting there doing sloth duty, waiting.

David finishes off his beer and heads over toward the pool. The kids are jumping in and splashing. He moves over and scoops up Mikayla as she laughs and squeals in delight. She puts her arms around his neck and then gives him a hard hug that reveals everything she feels about her daddy.

"Don't want to turn into an ol' prune 'fore your birthday, do ya?" David says as he nuzzles his nose against hers, ignoring that his clothes are getting wet. "The big day's less than a week away."

"I'm gonna be five," Mikayla declares to everybody around them.

David can't believe that she's going to be five. A year passes in a blink.

It was only yesterday that I was rocking her to sleep in my arms.

But he doesn't finish the thought. Rather, he embraces his little girl again, who isn't so little anymore. He recalls the other night when she had fallen asleep on the couch and he had carried her upstairs to her bed. In that moment, he had noticed just how much Mikayla had grown. Sometimes she didn't stay in place long enough for him to *really* notice.

David drapes a towel around her and then brings her to the table. As Mikayla dries off, David walks over to one of his favorite possessions: an antique record player in pristine condition. He carefully slides out a record and puts it on. The sweet chords of Smokey Robinson's "More Love" begin to play along with his one-of-a-kind voice.

It's the sound of summertime.

David turns up the speakers and doses everybody with a little more love.

He's a happy and lucky man and he wants to share that joy with everybody else.

—14—

As the song begins to play, Kari places more ice in the beer
bucket. She can't help but smile at the selection and the volume
of the song. Les quickly grabs another brew.

"Oh boy, there he goes. That dusty was before we all were born!"

Kari only nods at him, but enjoys listening to the familiar song.

"Need any help?" he asks as they're out of earshot from the rest
of the group.

"I think I've got it covered."

"Good, I didn't mean it anyway. I intend to thoroughly indulge
myself this weekend, even if I'm on call." He takes another sip and
almost half of the beer is gone. "Want one?"

"No, thanks," Kari says.

Les seems to watch her with curiosity.

"What do they say, Les?"

"Always has to be in control."

She nods and smiles, knowing there's a lot of truth in his comment. This is just another one of those comments Les has shared with
her and only her over the years. Slight, subtle, sometimes suggestive
comments that Kari knows enough to avoid. She avoids any more
conversation as she walks over to David, still by the record player.

"May I have this dance?" he asks.

"You may," she says, seeing that familiar boy-like grin on his
face—the one he's had ever since getting out of the shower and suddenly feeling like he was sixteen again.

David pulls her close to him.

"I love you," he says over Smokey's singing.

"Just happen to remember that?"

"Sometimes a man needs to remind himself how good his life is."

He gives her a kiss—soft and slow and gentle. It's probably the meal and the beer and the relaxing feel at the end of the day, but David lets the kiss linger for a while. Soon their friends all start hooting and hollering.

As the other couples get up to dance, David puts on another faster song to get everyone really moving.

"Whoo wee, okay now," Tia says. "That's my song!"

The sun is fading, but the party gets brighter and brighter.

—15—

Mikayla started sleeping in her big-girl bed just a month ago She lies surrounded by more than a dozen stuffed animals watching her as she closes her eyes and says her nightly prayer. Kari sits beside, holding her hand, while David stands at the door.

"Now I lay me down to sleep. I pray the Lord, my soul to keep. And if I die before I . . ."

Bold, brown eyes open as Mikayla sits up and faces her mommy.

"That's not good to think about," the child says.

Kari smiles, shooting a glace at David.

"Maybe you should make up your own prayers." She strokes Mikayla's hair, which is still a little wet from the bath. "Just remember— what's most important is that you know God's always watching you. He'll never let you down."

"What happens if you let God down?"

"He forgives you. Gods loves us no matter what."

Mikayla appears to be thinking about this. But, soon she shuts her eyes and says, "Bless everyone. Amen."

"That's it?" Kari asks.

David appears amused by the doorway. "Does seem to cover just about everything."

Mikayla tugs at her favorite purple blanket and pulls it over her, then moves onto one side facing the wall.

Kari kisses her good-night and looks at the Bible verse that they had painted on the wall in pretty calligraphy by a local artist:

"Children are a gift from the Lord."

She loves having this hanging over Mikayla, not that any of them need reminding, but rather as visible thanks to the Lord who made this precious little creature.

As she walks out, David comes in to tuck Mikayla in. All part of the nightly ritual. Kari can hear their conversation just outside the door.

"Sleep tight," Daddy says.

"Don't let the bed bugs bite."

"And if they do—"

"I'll hit 'em with a shoe."

"And make those bugs—"

"All black and blue."

Kari peeks in as David kisses Mikayla's forehead, then receives an-other big hug from the little girl. She isn't always as cooperative, but tonight is one of those nights where her sweetness shows through. David turns off the light.

"Night, Daddy."

The voice is pure and perfect.

"Sweet dreams, dawlin'," he answers.

– 16 –

The house is no longer being watched.

Now it's being approached.

The figure blends into the dark, the boots silent on the soft grass.

Night has come, but the dreams with it aren't always so sweet.

$-17-$

Some time later, when time has lost its significance, she can feel his steady breathing like the steady stroke of his hand. This is her David, when he's not worried or distracted, when he's not posturing or playing his man card. He's a satisfied lion curled up and intertwined with her in their bed. The ceiling fan purrs, serving as background noise as much as for the cool breeze.

David's hand caresses her arm, examining it in the semidarkness.

"I love this scar. It's kinda sexy . . . in a *bad* girl way."

Kari likes looking down on David, feeling like he'll do whatever she wants, whenever she wants it. "Oh, I can be *very* bad."

He chuckles softly. "Yeah, right."

Her head moves closer to his, the rest of the world far away, their eyes and lips so close. "Don't believe me, huh?"

"Kari—you feel bad if you miss choir rehearsal."

"Yeah, yeah, yeah," she says. "So you think you know me."

"I do, don't I?"

She brushes back her hair and gives him an enticing look. "Mystery can be good. It keeps a man on his toes."

"You're right about that . . . ," he says, using his toes to tickle hers.

For a moment, she thinks about the scar, and about all the other scars David doesn't know about and will never know about.

Leave the past in the past, Kari.

The domestic Kari, the responsible Kari, the motherly Kari—these are the sides of her that David knows. But the bad Kari—the out-of-control Kari—he can never meet.

"I was thinking about my mom at the barbecue today," David says, bringing Kari back to the present. "She loved some barbecue. I've been thinking about her a lot lately."

"I don't think anybody ever gets over losing their mother. They just learn to live with it." She looks in those deep eyes of his. "My mom would have loved you."

"So, you're saying your old man wouldn't have approved of me?"

"C'mon. How could he not have approved of you?"

David grins. "I know one thing—he would've loved my crawfish."

She leans over in bed and kisses him long and hard. "Anyway, we have our own family now."

"Do you ever think about adding on to our family?"

"Sometimes," Kari admits. "But then again, I sometimes just want to keep Mikayla this age forever. She's growing up so fast."

"Too fast."

–18–

The house has a heartbeat. The doors and windows are its veins, pumping life in and out.

Someone makes a brushing sound by a window. Unseen and unheard. A hand checks. Then the figure blending into the night continues to check.

There's always an open lock and an open window with a screen letting in some air. Always.

Letting in some cool night air and anything else the night might bring.

−19−

Kari has slipped her nightgown back on and is in his arms again, staring up at the ceiling, listening to him talk.

"Sometimes I wonder what would've happened if I hadn't met you."

She doesn't answer David simply because she doesn't understand the question.

"Let's face it: I'm a man infatuated with *ideas*. But you made me put down my books and breathed life into my world, into the life right in front of me."

When she looks at him, his gaze is raw and intense and real. Her knight in shining armor is wearing no armor right now. He's bare and she knows he loves her dearly.

"You saved me from my stupid self," he finishes.

He gives her a tender kiss, which reveals that he's not in the mood to go to bed, that he's not finished communicating with her.

"You saved me too David," she says, grateful that he can speak to her this way.

Something sounds in the hallway outside their door. She pulls away for a moment.

"Did you hear something?"

David sits up and listens for a moment. The door bolts open, startling both of them as the running figure of Mikayla launches herself into their bed.

"Baby, what's the matter?"

Mikayla is crying and breathing heavily. It takes her a few moments to talk clearly.

"I had a bad dream. The boogeyman was in my closet."

Kari holds her close. "Did Daddy leave that darn door open again?"

As David shrugs, she can tell that he's slipping back on his boxers underneath the covers. Kari attends to Mikayla's tears.

"I'd never let anything happen to you, darling," David says as he nestles beside her.

Mikayla is safe between her parents and is soon fast asleep.

Sleep doesn't come as fast for Kari. It never has.

$-20-$

Monsters hide in the dark, underneath beds and in the corners of closets. In the minds of children, fears come alive when the lights go out and imaginations run wild.

They all say that God's got a plan, claiming "It's God's will, Kari."
But sometimes you gotta change something deep inside in order to
figure out that plan and that will. I'd forgotten about that part of me.
But the sun risin' can shed light on any dark hole. Today it would
start to shine on mine.

ON THE FIRST DAY

— 1 —

Kari holds her car keys and knows they're already ten minutes late. Mikayla is still piddling around upstairs.

The sunlight bursting through the tall beveled-glass window in their foyer greets Kari with a warm hug like a close relative she sees every morning. With half a cup of coffee and half a muffin finished, she knows that they need to be on their way.

"Baby, we're gonna be late for school." Kari wipes some crumbs belonging to Mikayla's bagged lunch off her pantsuit.

David, an early riser since she first got to know him, has been gone for at least an hour. This is their regular weekday routine.

Kari thinks fondly of yesterday, a very full and very satisfying Sunday. Soon the busyness of the week will be in full gear and she'll be wishing it was Saturday again.

A sound above her makes her look up and see the figure in a dress appearing at the top of the stairs.

"Where's your coat, young lady?"

"I can't find it."

Letting out a sigh, Kari climbs the stairs.

The room is in order just like always. Mikayla takes after her, being a bit of a neat freak, as David likes to say. Someone has to clean up the house and David's not ever going to do it. She opens the closet door and finds the pile of clothes on the floor. She shoots Mikayla a look.

"It wasn't my fault."

"Excuse me?" Kari shakes her head.

"I'm not lying, Mommy."

She's about to say something, to drive home the point that there's no reason to lie, but the look on Mikayla's face causes her to stop.

She feels something she can't explain. An instinct kicks in, yet it's only for a split moment. The clock is ticking and they need to go.

"Come on," Kari tells Mikayla.

As she follows her daughter down the stairs, she thinks to call David.

− 2 −

Kari sits at her cubicle adorned with photos of the family visible from every side, and dials her husband's number.

"Hey, babe, what's up?" David says into his cell.

"Something weird happening this morning. Mikayla's closet was a total mess. That's unusual for her, especially since she claimed she didn't do it."

"I wouldn't worry about it," David says.

"Why would Mikayla do that to her own closet?"

"Kari . . . ," he says with a chuckle.

"What?"

"She was probably checking for the boogeyman and accidentally pulled down some hangers."

"It was dark," David continues. "And she was probably dreaming. Or maybe she was just getting back at you for being such a neat freak."

She knows he's just trying to lighten her mood.

Kari takes cash from her wallet and then slips it into a blank white envelope. She's counted it four times, six hundred dollars in twenty-dollar bills. She glances behind her, checking to make sure nobody is watching. The real estate office is usually quiet this time of the morning.

"I think we should install an alarm," she says as she seals the envelope. "I could have sworn I heard something last night."

"It was nothing. We don't need another monthly bill."

"I'll pay for it."

The laugh on the other side of the phone is a little too strong for her liking. "You haven't sold a house in months."

"For your information, I'm in multiple offers on the Morton place."

"Great! Then you can pop for an ESPN football package while you're at it."

"I don't think so."

"Hey—I gotta go," David says, his voice suddenly changing. "The students are getting restless and Beth just walked in."

"How's she doing?"

"Much better," he says.

"Poor thing," Kari says. "I can't imagine having to go through that alone. . . ."

David remains silent.

"Okay, I know you can't talk."

"Bingo," he says.

"See you at home."

— 3 —

Beth Hutchins is a twenty-four-year-old giving the impression of someone older despite her lean and long body. It's something in the way she holds herself, David has thought before. Something in those eyes doesn't back down.

"Jerold Whitaker wants to talk to *you*." She points toward David, then continues pointing at herself. "Not your 'damn teaching assistant.'"

David smiles, looking at her smooth caramel skin, her fitted blouse, and tailored suit. Dark green eyes. She is always easy on the eyes, he thinks.

"Still unhappy about his grade, or that you won't go out with him?"

Beth raises one eyebrow. "I'm not going out with *anyone* these days."

"I am sure there's some lucky guy out there just waiting to meet someone like you. If only you paid attention."

"I'm a woman surrounded by a bunch of boys," Beth says, then turning her gaze and body and getting his full attention before walking out the door again. "By the way, you're wearing that suit."

David smiles as she leaves the office and closes the door. But stops as his eye catches the picture of Kari and Mikayla on his desk. They're the beautiful women in his life, he says to himself. He doesn't need any more.

— 4 —

*Y*ou don't have to worry about a thing," Lemont once told her after first meeting him.

She was only sixteen, but she thought she was in love. She even carved his initials on her arm to prove it. The initials L. R. J. along with a heart. Lemont had liked that and had said he'd always be there for her, would always protect her, would always love her.

She didn't realize that Lemont's version of love also meant slapping her around or sometimes punching her in the gut. Or that there were others he loved too. That as she got older, there would be others who were younger that Lemont would start to prefer.

The tattoo on her arm had bonded them together. She would never get rid of it. The same way Lemont would never get rid of her.

But Lemont showed her something she was already beginning to know too well. Most men were monsters and only wanted one thing.

Especially in this part of the world, the part that wasn't so clean and so pristine and so prosperous.

A car honking brings Kari out of her daydream and reminds her that the light above her is green. She drives for a few more moments before arriving at her destination. Coming back here always reminds her. It's impossible for it not to.

The sprawling complex of three-story brick buildings gives the impression of a massive, fenced-in prison. They appear abandoned. The courtyards and sidewalks are empty. The grass is patchy with a lone tree sticking out every now and then. The gray sky seems to match the atmosphere of this housing project and Kari.

She knows the Iberville Projects well. Yet, like a horror movie she remembers seeing during her youth, the memories fade the older she becomes. The feelings, not so fast. Feeling a wave of goose bumps creeping over her skin, Kari pulls the SUV into one of the driveways and up in front of a building. The windows look back at her like judging strangers.

"Hello, ma'am?" the voice on the other end of her cell phone asks again.

Kari stops hearing the voices in her head and responds to the speaker, someone from the alarm company. "So Thursday's the earliest you can do the installation?"

"Yes, ma'am," the man says.

"Fine. Eleven a.m."

Kari exits her car and heads for unit six on the lower level. In her business suit, she couldn't stand out more. A couple of men smoking on the porch of another unit nearby just stare.

"Whatcha doin' around here, baby?" one of the men asks.

She ignores the comment and walks by them, knocking on the door that is her destination. After waiting for a minute with no answer, she slips the envelope underneath the door, then heads back to her vehicle. This has become a nasty habit she knows she won't be able to break.

The skinny hustler who had greeted her earlier smiles and reveals gold caps. "Don't ya got nothin' for me, honey?"

She looks them in the eye just to show them that they don't frighten her. She continues to her SUV and gets inside, already feeling dirty and in need of a good shower after having come back here.

In the silence of her car, Kari stares ahead at the open road, ignoring the buildings she's passing. She tries to drive as fast as she can to get away.

— 5 —

The lecture hall at Tulane University is full with students' faces aimed at David. He's popular with students at this school, which has been his work home for ten years. This is where he feels the most comfortable, standing here speaking to potential leaders of the next generation, sharing his ideas and ideals, posing questions such as, "Does the human condition change if humans themselves change?"

He lets the idea hover.

"When science vanquishes death, what will be the consequence if man no longer fears death?"

The door to the room opens and Beth enters, quietly taking a seat in the back like she so often does. As always, she is noticed by many of the males in this room.

He enjoys not simply stating opinions and theories and revelations. David loves asking questions to help illustrate and inform. Sometimes there is no one single answer to the great questions of life; you must ask them over and over again.

"One might argue that fearing one's demise serves a greater divine purpose. Namely, as a motivating factor to keep our behavior in check."

David glances and sees Beth look attentively like the rest of the students.

"For if man believes there is a karmic reckoning—be it God or the cold, harsh principle of cause and effect—this forces him to question the choices he makes in life. And is that not of value in itself?"

— 6 —

The smell of Mom's spaghetti sauce fills the kitchen and Mikayla waits. "You said we were gonna make cookies."

"You said you would stop eating treats before dinner," Mommy replies, then smiling adds, "Two more minutes."

Mikayla rides her scooter around the kitchen island as Mom watches her.

"That better not be a Hubig's I see in your mouth 'fore dinner?"

Mikayla laughs and rides out of the kitchen as she swallows. She knows that Mommy doesn't want her eating too many treats, especially after buying her an ice cream cone earlier this afternoon. But sometimes when Mommy is busy, she can get away with it.

She props her scooter on the edge of the couch and looks for something else to do. She'd like to watch Nick Jr. on television, but Mommy and Daddy don't like her watching *too* much television. She could go to the Nick Jr. website, but Mommy and Daddy don't like her messing around too much with the computer either. Mikayla thinks about asking Mommy if she can play on the computer anyway. But she instead heads down the hallway and notices the library door open.

Maybe Daddy's home.

She looks inside the office. Nobody is there. She feels a breeze and sees a window open, the curtains swaying next to it.

She knows that Mommy would never leave a window open. Mikayla's not worried. She never worries, especially in her house, where she's kept safe.

She heads to the window.

Maybe she'll climb out and then climb back in.

— 7 —

A parent cannot watch their child every waking moment.
And it can happen in just a second. That's all it takes.

Kari finished making the sauce and cleaning up the bowls and counters so she can start to make dessert with Mikayla.

"Cookie time!"

She doesn't hear Mikayla answer.

"Baby girl, I'm ready!" she calls out again.

Still no response. The house is large and sometimes Mikayla disappears into her room or into their bedroom playing with her dolls or reading a book or organizing her stuffed animals. Kari sighs.

She heads down the hall where Mikayla sometimes likes to play hide-and-seek.

"Mikayla?"

She goes into David's library since she sees the door open.

She looks downstairs.

"I'm going to find you," she says as she heads back upstairs with a fear familiar to every parent, especially every mother. Surely Mikayla is upstairs hiding. Or in the bathroom brushing her teeth with the water going full blast. Or maybe on the computer upstairs.

She checks all the usual spots. Mikayla's closet. The guest bathroom tub. The corner of their closet behind her long robes.

The prick becomes a cut.

Kari calls out for her daughter again, this time feeling an urgency inside of her.

"Mikayla, come on, I don't have time for this. Come on, where are you, sweetie?"

The tone in her voice is enough to get Mikayla's attention. But Mikayla still doesn't come out of hiding.

She checks upstairs, moving faster and faster, calling out her daughter's voice. Louder, more forceful and serious.

"Baby, where are you? Mommy's worried."

Panic starts to bubble like the red, hot sauce in the pot downstairs.

She goes back into David's library. The window's open.

Frozen in time, the figure standing at the entrance of the room is no longer Kari the terrified mom, but a small, hurt girl wanting to run away from this moment. She shivers, not because she's cold, but because she knows.

The curtain sways as if it's waving good-bye.

— 8 —

Kari calls the neighbors on either side, then David, and then the cops.

David rushes through the door. She falls into his arms. "I was in the kitchen, trying to finish up dinner so I could bake cookies with her. It was just a few minutes, David. I don't know how she disappeared from the house."

She continues to try to explain, but the words coming from her own mouth make no sense to her.

"Calm down. There's got to be an explanation. I'm sure Mikayla's fine."

The first officer arrives shortly after David, and she repeats everything to him. He asks her what she's wearing, what she was doing last, if they had been arguing, and if there were any serious medical issues. While the officer talks to Kari, another officer arrives, then a third car.

The next few moments blur by like some scary movie she's watching. A couple of detectives arrive along with forensic officers. She's asked permission to search the house. Another detective asks how the two of them are doing, which she doesn't even understand at first. The line of cars in their driveway seems to be growing by the moment.

Kari hears the sound of a dog and knows it's another tool to use in the search. David is talking to the cops and searching the house and making calls on his cell. She seems to be in slow motion, watching and waiting without being able to say much.

"Does she have a cell phone?"

"Did you contact all your friends in the neighborhood?"

"Have there been any unusual things happening around here?"

"How has she been at school?"

The list of questions by the police seems endless, all while the list of worries quickly starts building. Kari is mentally kicking herself for not getting the security system installed by now.

Neighbors on the street gather outside with their arms crossed and faces concerned. "What happened?" echoes in their chatter.

A couple of cops continue to ask Kari questions while trying to settle her down as well. More cops come and go through the front door. Soon Kari excuses herself to go find David, who is on his knees praying in his office. She has been so frantic that she hasn't stopped to pray, which is exactly what she does.

"Lord, please protect Mikayla and keep her from harm," Kari whispers in the room.

A cop enters just as the doorbell rings. Kari goes back to finally see familiar faces.

"Honey, you doin' okay?" Tia gives her a big hug as she walks in with Les.

Kari just embraces her friend and fights the tears. "I was just with her and then she was gone. Just like that."

Les doesn't appear to be distressed at all. Kari wonders if that's just the doctor in him, knowing he's able to handle bad news and adversity every day in his job. As David comes into the foyer, he sees the couple and embraces Les.

"She's going to be found," Les tells him.

They make their way to the kitchen where a couple of cops are talking.

"Listen—we've called everybody we can and we have them calling others," Les says. "If she's really missing, we have to act now. Call the media. Call Bishop Jakes and organize a search team among the team members."

Kari doesn't want to think so fast. Mikayla has been gone now for a couple of hours.

I can't think the worst. Not yet. Not now.

"Can you think of anywhere she might have gone?" Les asks.

"I've already answered that question half a dozen times." Kari knows her tone is defensive and tired. "She didn't wander off. She's too smart to do that and be gone this long."

"He's just trying to help," David says.

The faces looking back at her don't help her anxiety. They appear serious and critical, as if they're blaming her.

That's crazy, Kari tells herself.

But she is the one who was with Mikayla when she disappeared. She is the one responsible.

"We're going to find her and she's going to be okay," Tia tells her.

For the first time in a long time, Kari doesn't believe the reassuring words her friend says.

— 9 —

As the sun slips away, so does any hope that Mikayla might be simply hiding in the woods. The arrival of two more police cars seems to cement the terror.

Detective Gail Barrick has stood in a foyer of a home like this before for the very same reason. She doesn't want to be here, but knows that's what she gets paid to do, to stand and uncover the truth and to not let the hopeless terror seep into her veins like the oil in the Gulf. She needs to be strong for this family, because they're going to need every ounce of hope they can get.

God bless 'em.

Gail takes off her worn cowboy hat as she waits to hear what Frank has to say.

"Found a ratline outside the library window," the lean CSI officer says as he casually examines the interior of the entryway. "A man's size-eleven boot print."

Not what I wanted to hear, Frankie boy.

"Which would indicate Mikayla was carried off."

Frank gives a slow nod. The eccentric cop from the West Bank has seen his share too. Some get burned out. Some drink their way through it. And some, like Frank, seem to grow a little batty.

"Think it's the same guy the fellas on the West Bank been dealin' with?"

As Gail starts to answer, the cough seizes her and she barks into her hand for a few moments.

"Best take care of that Katrina cough," Frank says to her.

She nods at him, wiping her eyes and clearing her throat. "It's all the damn mold we got in N'awlins now. . . ."

He waits for her before they go into the living room to the Ameses.

"Last thing I need is another man trying to take care of me," Gail tells him.

"Not tryin' to take care of anybody. I just like seeing that pretty face of yours."

"You might be seein' a lot more of it if this goes the way I'm hoping it doesn't. Let's go talk to the parents."

$-10-$

Kari sits on the couch between David and Tia, but she feels like she's in the ocean, her arms outstretched and her body floating on the surface. She's wading lifeless in this massive body of water, with nowhere to swim to. The panic is engulfing her like water from a broken dam, pouring into her soul. She feels like every second that passes gets worse.

My baby, my sweet li'l baby.

"They'll find her," Tia tells her, holding her hand.

"You know how curious Mikayla is," David says. "She probably just wandered off."

Kari doesn't want to hear things others are supposed to say. The only thing that matters is hearing Mikayla's voice. Hearing her high-pitched laugh and seeing those bright eyes coming back through the door.

"An MCB just went out," Detective Barrick tells her.

The detective looks strong and tough, her dark skin and piercing eyes facing Kari. She guesses that Barrick has seen and heard everything. Something about the way she talks and holds herself speaks of a history there. A history not unlike her own.

"MCB?" David asks.

"Missing child bulletin."

Each word makes her hurt a little more.

They wait to hear the detective say more, but she doesn't.

"What is it?" Kari asks.

For a second she wants to know if this detective has any children, if she knows what it's like to be a mother, what it's like to have a little girl that's no longer there to hold.

The detective glances at her silent colleague standing next to her, then looks at Kari. "It's possible your daughter may have been abducted by M. K."

The wave propels her upward, then back down. Kari feels heavy and lifeless at the same time, spiraling uncontrollably, her mind clawing and gouging to get out, her soul quivering.

"The Merrero Killer?" David says.

The words vanish in smoke in this hollow room. Kari doesn't feel Tia's strong grip nor David's hand on her leg. She holds her face in her hands now and just wants to wake up.

"Every grab has occurred on the West Bank. Looks like this perp might have expanded his reach to Orleans Parish."

Kari remembers the poor woman on Sunday passing out a flyer about a missing child.

"Nothing's for certain yet," Tia says more to Kari than to the detective.

Kari wipes the tears and looks at Detective Barrick. "Maybe it's just someone else. Maybe Mikayla's been kidnapped. What's to say we won't get a phone call demanding ransom money?"

"The MO's the same, Mrs. Ames," the detective states.

She can hear the detective walk over to David, who is now standing.

"Would you and the wife mind comin' down to the station tomorrow?"

"Why?"

"We need to polygraph you."

Kari looks up, surprised by this statement. David's enraged.

"If you're insinuating that we had something to do with this . . ."

"You're not a suspect, Mr. Ames," the detective says. "But procedure dictates that we investigate the family as a formality."

"Yes. Yes. We just want our daughter back," David says.

"We want that for you too, sir," the detective says, seeing the fear in the man's eyes and in his wife, embraced by her friend.

God knew all I'd done to change, and that I'd never asked anything for myself. But today, I begged and pleaded. He'd already taken lots from me. This time, as I watched the sunrise without my baby girl at my side, I prayed He'd take from someone else.

ON THE SECOND DAY

— 1 —

D ear Lord, you know what I've done to change, to make myself more acceptable in your sight," Kari prays aloud, kneeling in her daughter's empty room, holding on to the covers of the child's bed. "Lord, our daughter, your child, our child is missing. And please, keep your arms around her, keep her safe, and bring her back home to us. Thank you, for she is on her way back to us now. Lord, please. I've done my best. Help us. Amen."

Outside their home, the placid surface of the pond water reflects the sky above—open, clear, and endless. This is what attracted the Ameses to this house in the first place. Now the tranquil pond that reflected the face of their child mirrors the images of police officers, a canine team, and volunteers walking the grounds to see if they can find any trace of the little girl who's been missing since yesterday evening.

A strange man walks among them, just a nobody with a big heart here to help out, looking for a lost girl. He wears sunglasses and a baseball cap—not unlike other men, do-gooders from in and out of their neighborhood. He doesn't look for any signs, however. He pays attention to those around him, to the men and women working and searching. He watches them from behind his shaded view.

"Take a look at this," a voice calls out not far from him.

Some young guy wanting to do his part and probably secretly wishing he could be a cop too. The volunteers wait as a policeman walks over to where he is. The man in the glasses and baseball cap decides to go over there too. He's curious.

Everybody sees the boot prints leading into the woods.

They act like this is a big discovery and that they're on to something.

But the man watching knows differently.

— 3 —

Kari wonders if God has pressed the mute button on her or if He keeps hearing her desperate pleas.

"Kari, time to go."

David's voice startles her. She opens her swollen eyes and turns around. Already she has grown skittish and spooked.

The David standing in the doorway in a shirt but no bow tie looks unlike himself, exhausted. The last time she can remember him appearing this way was after the birth of Mikayla, when he'd been up all night as well, but his face was joyful, not twisted by distress.

"Okay . . . a minute," she tells him in a whisper.

She opens the bedroom curtain and peeks outside at the growing circus on the street in front of their house. Several reporters with camera crews are parked outside, waiting to get their sound bites. Several squad cars are parked on the street as well as vehicles belonging to colleagues of David's or people from the country club. A part of her wants them all to just leave them alone. This is not their business nor their story. This is between David, Kari, Mikayla, and God. That's all. She doesn't have the energy to put on the smile and act the part. Not today. Not now.

She's been smiling and acting for a very long time.

Kari sighs.

She heads downstairs.

− 4 −

Kari's gaze keeps returning to a woman siting on a bench. Her hands are in cuffs and she's wearing a too-loose, too-sheer top and a skin-tight skirt revealing bruised and bony legs. No layer of fat to be seen, her cheeks protrude and her makeup looks smeared. She spots Kari.

"What you lookin' at, bitch?"

Kari doesn't have the energy to respond. She simply looks away.

"Mind your words, *chatte*," Detective Barrick says to the down-and-out woman. "Thank you for coming, Mrs. and Mr. Ames."

They stand and follow the detective. Kari looks again and feels a tinge of sadness at the hardened woman and wishes she could help her in some small way.

"You guys know how this works, right?"

Barrick is no-nonsense and to the point. She doesn't appear to be the hand-holding type.

"Can't say I'm being grilled on a polygraph all the time," David says.

"You've seen cop shows, right? This monitors things like your breathing and blood pressure. Just tell the truth and we'll be all good. Mrs. Ames, would you like to go first?"

Kari nods. The examiner is a bald and nonexpressive man who asks her a few basic questions before hooking her up to the machine. A blood-pressure cuff goes around her arm while a pneumograph goes around her chest. The man conducting the interview sits next to her in a chair with a computer in front of him. Part of her feels like this can't be happening, that she's in some comedy and that Mikayla is going to jump out any minute with a *Surprise, Mommy*.

If only that were true.

For a second, she thinks of what she read online about polygraph tests, specifically the article about what to do when taking a polygraph test.

"Answer yes or no. Understand?"

She nods at Mr. Not-So-Friendly as he glances at his computer and then at the notes in front of him. Kari can't help but think of the face of the streetwalker on the bench. She wonders how old the woman is, but thinks she has to only be in her early twenties if that.

"You currently reside at 1135 Cheverly Avenue. Correct?"

"Yes," Kari says.

"Your name is Kari Ames."

"Yes."

"Your daughter was born in 1985."

She can't help but flex her wrist to try and feel the sensation in it. "No."

The questions continue. She stares ahead, focused and steady. When the questions come she answers almost mindlessly.

"I don't know where my daughter is."

"I had nothing to do with her being gone."

"No."

"Yes."

"No."

"Yes."

"No."

She feels the slow fingernails of time scratching against her soul, making her anxious about the ticking time and all the things she could be doing instead of answering these stupid questions.

— 5 —

As Kari gets her polygraph, the detective briefs David on their progress in searching for Mikayla.

"We've contacted everybody in the neighborhood, all of the families at her school and at the church. Even all the relatives. Nobody has any leads on where Mikayla might be, but they now know to be on alert. Many of those families are assisting even now in searching for her."

David studies the deep lines on the detective's face. "Do you have people looking for her now?"

"We've had cops out there all night. Search parties. We've gone through the house. Checked phone calls and emails. We've sent out alerts to neighboring towns and counties."

"What about one of those AMBER alerts?"

"That can only be sent when we know the child has been abducted."

"So what are we supposed to do in the meantime? Just go about our business, sit by the phone, and wait for your call?"

"I'm sending my team over to tap your phone line," Detective Barrick says. "You need to be patient. I know it's easier said than done—"

"Patient? You and I both know that every hour that goes by decreases Mikayla's chances of survival."

Barrick doesn't react in any way to his words. He's about to say more when Kari walks into the office. David stands, grabbing her hand. "Come on, honey, let's get out of here."

— 6 —

Mikayla sits in the silent darkness, on the hard cement floor of an empty closet. She's cried so much already, the tears now come in fits and spurts. Crying's not going to get her anything.

Mikayla now talks to her teddy bear to stay busy. She tries to talk in a normal voice, but she can't help but whimper and close her eyes. Wanting to just wake up. Wanting to just wake up and see her mommy and daddy.

She needs to be strong. She's heard her mommy say that before. She remembers that and thinks about it and tries to be a big girl like Mommy.

The sound of footsteps slowly descending. There's a creak in the steps just like last time, door opening. Then the sound of keys.

The scary feeling comes again.

The closet door opens and a blast of light causes Mikayla to squint and cower in the corner. She hears the shuffle of movement and then of something placed on the floor. For a moment she feels watched. Then the door squeaks and closes and she is left alone.

The steps go back up the stairs.

"I want my mommy," she yells out. "I want my mommy."

Soon she stops shouting and feels around for what was left for her: a sandwich, something crunchy like potato chips, something square with a straw—a juice box.

Even though her mouth waters and her tummy rumbles, she doesn't eat the food, but rather puts her arms around herself to keep from being so cold.

She recites the prayer she would pray with Mommy and Daddy. Over. And over. And over again.

— 7 —

Kari grips her wrist with her other hand to try and stop the shaking while keeping both on her lap, hidden from David's view.

At times she feels hot all over, then next she feels cold as if the blood in parts of her body has stopped circulating. The world spins around ten times faster than normal. The car feels like a prison cell, while the outside haunts and taunts her. David drives down a street toward their house and she spots a shrine to a dead soul. A circle of lit candles and crosses and pictures of a dark-skinned smiling boy surrounded by images of saints. A crowd stands as if waiting for the boy to return, as if hopeful that the streetside vigil will be enough to sway God to return this lost son.

David sees this and shakes his head, not saying anything.

A group of women there are weeping, standing around a woman dancing—a voodoo priestess. Seeing the sight fills Kari with dread. She turns her head.

"Two minutes," she says as if David isn't even in the car. "That's all it took."

"Kari . . ."

"Two minutes is all it took for our lives to change forever. If Mikayla had stayed in the kitchen with me. If she had just—just stayed. All she wanted to do was make cookies."

She feels as if she's falling.

"Right now I'd be picking her up from school. Then we'd go get frozen yogurt or stop by the park—"

"Kari," David says with a hand touching her leg. "It's not your fault."

Kari swallows, but her mouth is dry.

"She was with me. *I'm* the one who was looking after her. I should've made those alarm people come out that same day. Why didn't I listen to myself?"

"You can't start thinking of everything that you should've done," David says.

Kari nods.

As they approach their home a horde of media is there, anticipating their arrival.

David curses quietly as he slows the car down, unsure about pulling into the driveway. The masses converge on them like the Red Sea falling onto the Egyptians. Kari wants to slide down into the floor under her, but remains solid in her seat.

She doesn't want to leave David's side. Nor the sanctuary their Lexus temporarily provides.

— 8 —

The smiling couple exits the doors of their expensive car to strut past and slide back into their sweet, sensible life.

A reporter asks how they're holding up.

Another asks why they were at the police station.

Another asks if the police think their daughter was taken by the man known as "M. K."

As the questions continue without answer, the man snaps pictures without them knowing or seeing or having any idea.

He's just another figure in the crowd, wanting the right picture of the horrified family.

He's not the only monster surrounding the Ameses. He's just the only one who has the heart to act on the impulses that he sees deep in the well of his soul.

The expensive camera clicks off shots like a clock ticking off the remaining seconds of a little girl's life.

Someone carrying a plate of food bumps into Kari and then embarrassingly apologizes as she tries to make it into her kitchen full of people. She looks behind her and realizes the man is from her church. The woman he's standing next to is familiar to Kari, but not someone she really knows. It looks like there's a party going on in this house, with people standing and sipping coffee and talking. There are friends from their country club, colleagues from Tulane, and people from the church, all downstairs trying to do something.

For a second, the room looks like a snapshot of their last party. When the world felt better and brighter.

She braces herself to be strong in front of all her friends. Tia and Grace head toward her the moment she enters the room.

"How are you holding up?" Tia asks.

Kari nods. Tia hands her a paper.

"I wanted you to look this over before we make copies," Tia says.

Glancing at yet another flyer, she sees Mikayla's sweet, innocent face smiling. The grin gets to her like a slap on the face. Above her picture is the word "Missing" and below is "$50,000 Reward for Her Safe Return."

"Fifty grand?" Kari asks.

"Some of us got together on this. It was the least we could do," Pam says.

Grace motions over to the kitchen, where Beth is standing, entertaining Tia's six-year-old son. "Beth did the flyer on her Mac."

Her head dizzy and her voice weak, all Kari can say is "Thank you."

Beth nods and gives her a sad, empathetic look. If she was closer she'd probably give Kari a hug.

She glances at Pam holding a cup of coffee. At Tia explaining something to Grace. At Beth making Benjamin laugh. Ordinary people doing ordinary things. That's what's wrong with this picture. Because there's nothing ordinary about this day and about this house. And anything that does look ordinary needs to go.

I want to run down the streets and pound on doors and nail these flyers to the walls, Kari thinks. *Then I want to nail the creep who took Mikayla to the same damned wall.*

David approaches her and then pulls her aside.

"Look, Les gave me some Xanax. Maybe it'll help you rest."

Something about the way he says *rest* makes something inside of her snap. "I don't want to *rest*. You wanna take a pill—that's up to you. But I'm keeping my senses till we find our daughter."

David holds up a hand as if to say *Okay, all right* and to silence her. All these bodies and faces and voices are circling around her, making her dizzy. She feels light and heavy at the same time. She tries to say something else, but her mouth is still dry and her tongue seems stuck.

"Can I get you something?" a voice that sounds like Pam's says on her left.

"Folks been stopping by with food all day," another voice that sounds like Grace's says on her right.

She wants to close her eyes and wish all of them away. The sight of the faces staring at her, some trying to act nonchalant, others acting like they just saw death walk through the front doors. The smell of gumbo or black beans and rice or any number of other dishes that make her think of sweet laughter and sweet home. Even the soft touch of her friends and family, who only want to help.

"Why don't you go upstairs?" Tia says, gently taking her arm and then guiding her like a mom might guide her child.

Everybody stares at her as Tia guides her toward the stairs. She knows they can't help it. She would stare herself if this was happening to Tia or Grace or anybody else. The conversation seems a little quieter than when she first walked into the kitchen.

Before she leaves the room, she sees Les and Wayne leaning over and talking to Beth in a way that appears like they're comforting her. Les puts his arm around the anxious woman. Kari finds this odd, but realizes that David's teaching assistant is probably just shaken up like everybody else.

"Come on," Tia urges.

Soon Kari finds herself sitting on the edge of her bed in her silent bedroom. Tia shuts the door and then comes to Kari's side. Her friend looks like she's dressed for church.

"You're not gonna leave me, are you?" Kari asks.

Tia shakes her head. Her soft brown eyes soothe Kari's soul. "I'm here as long as you need me."

Tia kneels and gently removes Kari's shoes, then she stands and pulls down one of the sides of the bedspread. "C'mon, honey—just lie down and close your eyes. Just for a couple of minutes."

Kari just sits there, facing her dresser. She doesn't want to rest even though she barely slept at all last night.

"Kari, you can't do Mikayla any good if you're not rested and thinking straight. You just stay here," Tia tells her. "I'll be right over there in the armchair so no one bothers you."

Kari nods. "You're a good friend. I don't know what I would do without you."

"Don't worry about that. I'm not going anywhere."

The comfort of the bed and the warmth of the blanket can't make up for the cold, hard reality that has one arm around her chest and another around her throat.

–10–

This was the way life was supposed to work, David thinks.

Something happens and you make a call. You get someone on the line and he makes some calls. It's called who you know. It's about pulling strings. It's about helping out those who help you out. It's about influence.

David stands on his recently cut back lawn listening to the sound of the birds. This is better than the meaningless chatter on his phone. He wants to take it and whip it against someone's head.

"Everything possible isn't enough," he says in a controlled volume, knowing the others are still inside. "I don't give a damn about your budget. Mayor, the FBI needs to be involved. Now, not later."

The voice on the other end makes excuses, a soft response from a soft man. *A soft man in a soft life,* David thinks.

"Damnit, listen to me," David says. "This is my little girl missing. DO YOU HEAR ME? My friends and I got you elected. Don't make us regret it."

David ends the call.

David looks at the pool and remembers Mikayla's laughter when they were last in the water together. "I'm gonna be five," she had said in such a proud voice.

Then he thinks about the time Mikayla overheard them talking about a man on the news who had been convicted of abducting a child. She couldn't understand what the man had done, but Mikayla understood that this was a bad person.

"Maybe he just doesn't have any friends," she said in that innocent, loving way.

The memory punches him in his gut. Once again, tears are on the verge of spilling out.

For a moment, the question of why God would allow this to happen starts to seep in. The question of fault and blame suddenly come to mind.

I can't go there, he thinks, knowing these are dangerous thoughts.

Now is not the time to reflect and remember, David says to himself. *Now is the time to act.*

— 11 —

There is an order for everything on her desk, but Detective Barrick is the only one who could ever figure that out. In the middle of stacks of reports, files, more reports, coffee mugs, and pictures of family, a paper readout sits with all of its information waiting to be studied.

Ben tossed the printout for Mikayla's case on Detective Barrick's desk just a few minutes ago, waiting for her to make sense out of it. For a second she wonders if he's trying to test her knowledge of the polygraph reports. She doesn't have time to try to decipher everything, so she just glares at him, demanding an explanation.

"Check out these biometrics on the Ames polygraph," Ben says gesturing with his hands toward the document. "A tad irregular, huh, sugar?"

The detective nods. "I'll say."

"Wait—there's more."

He lays a file on her desk. She rifles through it, each page surprising her a little more. Barrick eventually closes it and sighs.

She wanted to believe that she wasn't going to find any skeletons in the family closet. But unfortunately, every family has them. And some of those skeletons eventually escape.

"Looks like I need to pay the Ameses another visit."

−12−

Day becomes dark and the crowd at the Ameses' house finally disperses. Kari is lost in the computer screen, searching for a key.

But what she sees are ten millions pictures of the bruised and the broken.

She first types in "Missing Girls New Orleans" into Google. Then she begins to filter and sort from there. She finds a year-old article, prints it out, then finds another dated from this year. She reads them and then skips over to another article or headline, reading, printing, reading more, clicking more.

So many can get lost and maybe some found. All through the help of this wonderful thing known as the Internet.

Reading the stories adds to her terror. After an hour or maybe even longer, Kari begins to sort back through the printed pages in her hands. She organizes them chronologically, then begins making notes.

Twenty minutes into the process she gasps and stands to go find David.

He's in the silence of the family room, standing by the window, peering out the custom-made wood shutters.

She calls his name, yet he doesn't budge.

"There's only two left," David says. "I wish these reporters would just leave us alone."

His broad shoulders look tense, the way they might after a long day of classes. Normally she would make him sit in his favorite chair and then grind out the stress with her strong palms.

This isn't one of those times.

He turns to face her. "What happened?"

"Every little girl M. K. abducted was found dead on the *sixth* day."

The vice of controlled anger and tension filling David seem to vanish in a second. He suddenly looks like a deflated, gray balloon.

"Why didn't the police say anything?" she continues.

His eyes move downward, his voice unable to say anything.

Before he can respond, the doorbell announces someone or something. They both glance at each other.

"Don't answer it," she tells him.

"We need to see who it is."

"It's probably just another reporter wanting to know some more gossip to print."

David doesn't say anything as he glances through the peephole, then looks back down at Kari.

"It's the police," he says.

Detective Barrick's somber face waits at their entryway. Behind her are two men who must be fellow cops.

Please . . . Kari says to herself, not uttering a word aloud. She refuses to finish the sentence.

"As far as we know, your daughter is still alive, Mrs. Ames," Barrick says. "Do you mind if my guys get to work on that phone line?"

"No . . . of course, go ahead."

The men step inside to the main entry of the house, where a chandelier hangs over them bursting in bright light. Kari can see the tough lines on the woman's face, etched wrinkles on the dark skin from years of police work. She imagines that the detective was once a pretty young lady before the damages of the job started to show.

"Why didn't you tell us?" Kari says.

"Tell you what?"

"That Mikayla has five days left."

Barrick's eyes quickly shift to David's.

"We didn't wanna worry you any more than necessary."

"Why are you here? You should be out there looking for her."

"Kari . . ." David puts a hand on her shoulder.

"I thought we might talk in private," Barrick calmly says to Kari. David looks puzzled.

"Private? Whatever you have to say, you can say in front of my husband," she tells the detective.

"Just tryin' to be respectful."

"Then get to the point."

"You think someone we know took Mikayla?" David asks.

Kari is looking at him through the eyes of someone else. This scene in front of her belongs to someone else. It's not happening to her—not here, not now.

The detective continues to look at her with suspicious eyes.

"Someone from Baton Rouge?" Barrick asks.

For a moment that feels like forever, Kari and the detective just stare at one another.

"Kari," David asks, "what's going on?"

The air racing around her is the sound of her falling off a cliff. She always feared that one day this moment would arrive.

"What's she talking about?" David asks again.

Kari says nothing, but her thoughts are loud and bouncing around inside her head.

The detective lets another minute pass before speaking. "Okay, we'll do it this way."

"Mikayla Carter: two years in the women's correctional institute for narcotics possession—"

"Who's Mikayla Carter?" David says in a voice wanting an answer.

"Eight months for prostitution. Nine weeks for battery. Another five for petty theft." Those dark Creole eyes stare back at Kari. "Just tell me you want me to stop."

"I'm a different person now."

"You're a different person . . . *now*?" David says, looking like he's seen a ghost. "Mikayla Carter—is that you?"

Her silence answers. "Mrs. Ames, if someone has it out for you, now would be the time to tell me."

Kari just remains silent, holding back the ocean of rage that's twisting inside of her.

"I'm only trying to help here," Barrick says, seeing her look. "With a rap sheet like yours—I have to ask. Have you talked to anyone or seen anybody from your past?"

"No, I have not and unless I'm a suspect or you have new information about our daughter, you should leave."

"Well, if anybody comes to mind, call me." For a moment it looks like the detective is going to say more, but she knows that she's said enough. She nods and then turns around to exit.

Kari watches the door shut. She locks the bolt and then looks for David. He's slipped back into the family room, where he's sitting on the couch looking even more lost than ever.

He doesn't even glance her way as she moves closer to him. She stands at the couch they picked out together, feeling its expensive fabric against her rough hands.

"What is going on?" David asks, his mind clearly still trying to figure out what it just heard.

"This doesn't have anything to do with my past."

"You lied to me." David's voice is the voice of a stranger, lost and searching for a home.

"It wasn't a lie. I kept secrets. I thought if I changed my name, my old life would go away."

"Who are you? Are you going to tell me now?"

"David, this is not the time to go into this."

"Don't you think you'd better tell me? Given that the police know and soon everyone else will as well."

This is not the sort of reply she would have imagined. It has nothing to do with Mikayla. Hell, it has nothing to do with her.

It's about the appearance of things.

"Would you get out of your self-pity and your fear of losing your stupid status?" she yells. "I don't care what anyone thinks of me, of us right now. I want my daughter back."

"She's my daughter too, damnit. How do we know someone from your past didn't snatch her?"

"Because nobody knows where I am," she says, telling the truth. Or mostly the truth. "I left that life behind."

"How can you be so certain?"

"I am very certain. The moment I stepped foot onto the university campus and began a new life, I was certain. I didn't plan on things to happen like they did. I didn't plan on us."

"Why didn't you just tell me?" David asks.

"If you'd known my history, would you have given me a chance?" Kari asks.

The hurt and betrayal in his eyes has turned to a wildfire. David stands and grabs a framed shot from their wedding day and slams it against the table, cracking it in half. She sits on the edge of the couch, closing her eyes as she starts to cry.

"God is punishing me, I know it," she says, not to David but out loud to herself.

"Maybe you deserve to be punished."

"Because I would have done anything to erase who I was. Anything."

He doesn't respond.

She shakes her head. "I had a reason for acting out the way I did."

"Are you gonna tell me the reason or is that another secret you're gonna keep from me?"

"Do you really want to know?" she asks him, knowing the truth.

The truth is that David doesn't really want to know.

"I deserve to know what happened to you—what happened to my wife."

"I lost my mother at a young age. And after that, everything just— everything fell apart. With my life and with my father. Everything turned bad."

"How? Did he hurt you?"

"My father didn't have anybody else in his life except me. His little girl who was growing into a woman. I didn't have the time to figure out what that meant. Because he took whatever was left in the little girl—he took whatever innocence was still there. And he kept taking over and over and over again."

David just looks at her, his face a mixture of surprise and anger.

"Kari—"

"I was raped by my father. The things I had to endure . . . Nobody needs to relive them. I buried the past with my father. With that girl he ruined."

Something shifted inside David, hearing this. He fell silent again, overwhelmed by all these revelations.

"I knew you wouldn't want to hear the truth."

"It's not that. Why did you feel you couldn't tell me that? I'm your husband."

"You fell in love with some pretty young woman in your class. I wanted to be that person."

"So who are you?" David asks. "Really?"

"I don't know."

She bends over and picks up half of the broken frame on the floor. Yet there are too many pieces and they're scattered all over.

"All those times I used to ask about your family and about where you grew up—they were just lies?"

"I just didn't fill in the blanks," Kari says. "I told you I was estranged from my family. And it's true."

"How can you say something is true."

"You don't have to believe me. It doesn't matter. What matters is our daughter."

"Your past could be connected to Mikayla's disappearance," David says.

"Now you're blaming me for this?"

"How could I blame you? I don't even know you. Of the people you were dealing with, is there someone who might want to seek revenge or something?"

She wants to say absolutely not. Yet Kari knows she can't.

"I don't know." She holds her head in her hands.

He leaves the room and heads out the door.

"David . . ."

He goes to sit on the porch. Kari stands there by the window for a long time, paralyzed and unable to move or feel or think.

Then she turns off the light and heads upstairs, her fingers throbbing from the slight cuts from the broken glass.

She can hear David's car leaving before she's made it to the top step.

$-13-$

David calls Les and tells him he's coming over. When he arrives at his friend's house, David decides to tell him the truth. *That's what I want now: simple and uncomplicated.*

"Man, I just need to sit with you a bit. My wife. I don't know what to say, but I've found out some things that are just unbelievable."

"David, it's all right. Sit down. Rest yourself. I was just watching some TV."

Thankfully Tia isn't around to ask what's wrong. For a moment, David thinks that maybe Kari's already spoken to her. Les flips through the channels and stops at a newscaster reporting that Crime Stoppers is offering a reward for anyone who finds Mikayla.

"Good," Les says in the family room as they watch the flat screen television. "We should see some action now. For that kind of reward, somebody's gonna talk."

"I just pray we find her alive," David says, his forehead dotted with sweat even though it's not hot inside here.

"Don't even think that way." The look Les gives him is meant to encourage, but David knows Les is surely feeling the same way.

"Les, my wife's not the person I thought I married. She had a whole other kind of life before me that I'm just hearing about now. And I heard about it from the police."

Les doesn't barrage him with questions, which is good. It seems like he knows to just leave the specifics out of this conversation.

"Look, I don't know the details you're talking about, David, but

I know there's always been something about your wife that I could never put my finger on. A mystery. How are you gonna deal with it?"

David doesn't respond, initially surprised by Les's admonition yet also knowing his friend is just being honest.

"Did she have something to do with Mikayla's disappearance?" Les asks.

"I don't know," David says in a weary voice. "She's been through a lot, but she shouldn't have kept it from me."

"If I found out something like that about Tia, I'd have to kick her to the curb."

David looks over to his friend. "It's easy to say what you *would* do. But this is now. I loved Kari enough to marry her and . . . she's the mother of my child, Les."

"Well, be careful, my brother. You need to find out who you're married to and what her life was before you, so it doesn't come back to bite you again."

David nods and continues to stare ahead.

"I'm just saying, David—a seedy past, a bunch of secrets—this woman's gonna take you down."

It's too much to think about, too much to deal with. "I'll deal with her later. First, I've got to find my daughter."

−14−

All she can hear are the clicks of her heels against the dark hall-way floor. The night classes are over and she's finally finished with her work.

Her load is heavier than usual. But, that's okay. Anything she can do for David, she will. Even if it means staying late enough to make these ordinary hallways begin to look menacing and creepy. She wants to prove how valuable and stable she can be and always will be. She's a rock and men need a rock in their lives, no matter what's going on in it.

Her neck is sore and her mind is numb from reading, but she's still wide awake, wondering what's going on with the Ameses right now. The question has hovered around her all day, since stopping by the house earlier.

She opens David's office door and sees a figure sitting by the desk in the dark.

Beth gasps and clutches her papers. It's David.

"You scared me."

As she turns on the lights, his subdued voice says "Keep it off."

She's heard this tone before. Beth nods and then flicks off the switch.

"These midterms are all graded. I'll just leave 'em here."

She sets them on his desk and tries to make out his expression in the shadows. She can't see anything except the outline of a stationary profile.

There are so many things she wants to tell this man right now. So many things she wants to help him deal with.

He just needs time, Beth thinks.

She turns around and slowly begins to walk out.

"I don't give a damn about midterms or anything else right now," David shouts out. "I've combed every block within a twenty-mile radius of my home, rung every bell—nothing."

She stops and turns, trying to imagine his frustrations and fears. For a while he just stares at her.

"I can't begin to imagine what you're going through," Beth finally says. "If you need anything, just ask and I can take care of it. If you want me to take over your lectures—I know almost every word by heart."

She hopes he sees or at least senses that she understands. In the darkness, she can see him nod.

"I can't sleep," David says softly. "I can't turn my mind off. I just keep wondering . . ."

"They'll find her, I know they will. Mikayla's going to be fine."

He sighs, but says nothing.

"Do you want me to stay a while?" she asks.

There is a pause. Just a slight one, but noticeable nonetheless.

"No—it's late. Go on home."

Beth knows he will need her eventually, and she knows she will be there. Whatever happens in the end, she will be strong for this man.

She feels there's a part of this man she can heal, right here and now, but she knows it's not the right time. She turns and walks out of the office, leaving David behind her in silent darkness.

— 15 —

The cough seizes Barrick's throat. She drains the day-old coffee that's been fermenting in the cup on her desk. It does the trick, at least for the moment.

She and Frank have been mulling over the Ames situation. But, she feels like they've gotten no further than they were a couple of hours ago.

"Far as I can tell, Kari Ames has a clean sheet since leavin' Baton Rouge eleven years ago." Barrick taps the coffee cup and tries to make sense of the facts swirling around in her head.

The CSI officer wrinkles his face, making it even more ugly than usual. "Don't rule out a ghost creepin' up from her past."

She nods, knowing there are very few optimists working on the force, especially down here. She glances back down at the files on her desk. She can hear Frank adjust in his seat.

"Worst kinda enemy is the one you never see comin', sugar," she tells him.

"But then again, if this was revenge, the Ameses would've heard from someone by now," Frank says.

"True, but we still need to check out her past. You and the boys get started on that. In the meantime, I'm gonna shake down the local pervs. God knows there're enough freaks in this town for me to go door-to-door all night."

Frank once again agrees with her, yet settles back in his chair as if content to let the day be done. She stands up.

"Where you gonna start?" he asks.

"Ed Lainer. Lives a block from the Ames house."

—16—

Kari can't sit still. Every moment is a wasted opportunity. Every second passing is one more that's gone, one more that she can't get back. Even though researching articles online and printing them out, highlighting them, and taping them to the wall might not be the best thing for someone like her to do, it's something. It's doing something.

She has all the lights on in the house. Maybe if it's bright enough Mikayla can find her way back home even in the darkest of nights.

The voices tempt and mock, voices from long ago, faces and hands and whispers all belonging to strangers, all belonging to those who took. And took. And took.

She gets an idea from an article she printed off the web about a murder victim who was found days after disappearing. She's highlighted all the relevant details the way any officer or detective might. She's seen enough cop shows to know how to do this.

Her laptop is open alongside a stack of printouts on the coffee table. There are pictures of the victims, innocent and precious little faces.

Her family room has been transformed into a makeshift situation room. She's gotten a map of East Bank and taped it to the wall, sticking red pins in it where the victims have disappeared.

All those red pins everywhere feel like they're piercing her soul.

The information and the ticking clock and the details with nothing to do soon get the best of her. Kari knows she needs to talk with someone, and that someone is Tia. She grabs the phone. God knows where David is right now. She needs to hear something other than these voices in her head.

When the voicemail picks up, Kari hangs up.

The room seems to swirl around like a carousel ride. For a second, Kari closes her eyes, but she doesn't like the images that she sees. She can picture Mikayla's sweet smile, her bright eyes, her little life looking back at her. Kari forces her eyes back open and then stares at the clock.

She immediately goes to the liquor cabinet, picking up the bottle of expensive vodka and pouring a shot. She knows what it will do. It's been long, but it hasn't been *that* long. She knows that it will take a second to tilt her head and drain the clear liquid, and that it will take just another second for the liquid to start to clear her head.

You don't need this anymore, she tells herself.

For a moment she holds the glass and looks at the drink. Then she pours it into the sink.

—17—

Kari thinks to retrace what she imagines were Mikayla's last steps through the house. She ends up in David's library, looking at the ornate furniture and the dark wood. Her eyes scan the walls, the floors, the corners, every inch they can.

She goes into the garage and then comes back with a heavy hammer, which looks barely used, and the longest nails she could find. She begins to pound the nails into the window frame, hoping to keep the window from being able to open anymore.

But on her third nail, Kari realizes that she's wrong. For a moment she pauses, hearing something behind her. David is standing at the entrance to the room, his steady, piercing gaze cutting into her.

Before she gets back to work, a haunting revelation hits her. She glances at the window, then back at David.

"Why didn't she scream when he took her?" Kari asks him.

David's look of surprise evaporates into a look of deliberation.

Her mind is like a galloping horse sprinting to the finish line, oblivious of all the other horses around it.

"Seventeen sex offenders live within two miles of our home—did you know that?"

David just stares at her, not reacting at all to her questions, only feet away from her but not really there.

"Why out of all the children possible?" he asks.

She stops and tries to understand his question.

"Our daughter," he says. "Why'd you give her the same name?"

This isn't what she hoped he would say right now. The man is standing staring at her like a stranger, asking questions like the cops.

"So she could have the childhood I never did."

He just gives her a blank, uncaring stare.

She always hoped that one day she could tell David, that the truth could slowly be revealed in her own time and in her own way. But now is not the time. Kari knows there's no time to explain things. No time and no way.

David leaves. Kari doesn't hesitate as she resumes nailing without any interference from her husband.

—18—

When the phone rings again, Tia's heart sinks. She knew the moment Les found out about Kari's past, their friendship was over. Each ring sounds louder than the last. Finally, when her voice goes off in the bedroom, it seems to mock her fear of answering.

"Tia, call me when you get this," Kari's desperate voice says. "Doesn't matter what time. I need to talk to you."

Tia looks at her husband, who responds with a shake of his head.

"I don't want you to have anything to do with her," Les says. "She's trouble."

"She's my friend, Les."

"Your friend is trouble. I bet she's a ho and a drug addict. That's what she is. I'm not gonna allow her to ruin our lives like she has David's."

In the sanctuary of their mansion, the silence feels like a punishment. Tia knows she has to be there for her friend, yet she also realizes that she has to do what Les says. This house and this life they lead—it doesn't work without him.

"Maybe we don't know the whole story," Tia says.

"I know enough to know we're staying away from her. End of story."

$-19-$

Kari climbs the steps and thinks about forty-eight hours earlier, when she and David danced for everybody to the sweet sounds of Smokey Robinson and the Miracles.

As she heads up the familiar stairs, she avoids looking at the large family portrait. Now she can't stomach to see Mikayla in between her parents, just grinning and being as giddy as she can be.

As she enters their bedroom, the cover is still untouched. They've slept everywhere in the house—or tried to sleep—except with each other. She checks the guest bedroom and finds the door locked.

"David, are you in there?"

"I need to be alone right now."

The bed is their sanctuary, their security, their special place where only the two of them can go. Perhaps somehow, in some way, they can get something back if they just lie there next to one another.

Kari waits for an eternal moment, standing in the shadows of this large but empty house, waiting on this door to open and hoping loving arms will finally embrace her again.

The roar of silence in this room is like a lion waiting to devour her.

$-20-$

The house looks as run down as the ones on each side of it—a tiny residence in the armpit of nowhere with people trying to make their way through life without any more hardship.

Detective Barrick knocks on a door that resembles a wrinkled old man. A droopy-eyed girl probably in college answers the door. She doesn't look like she just woke up, and she doesn't look particularly surprised to see the woman standing there showing her a badge.

"Can I come in?" she says out of habit.

The girl is tall and skinny and she shrugs her bony shoulders.

"Why, thank you," Barrick says as she starts to walk through the doorway. "I'll take that as a yes."

"Ed around?" she asks the girl before she can protest the intrusion.

"He's asleep," the student says with the worst lie Barrick's ever heard. "You mind telling me what this is about?"

"Finish your homework. I won't be long."

Just her presence alone is enough to bully this tiny, weak young girl. Barrick walks down a hallway with bare, abandoned walls and a missing bulb overhead. She moves quickly but quietly, making sure good ol' Ed doesn't hear her coming.

The door at the end of the hallway doesn't have any light coming from the crack at the bottom. She turns the knob with a gentle grip, but finds it's locked.

She takes a step back and then rams through the door with her side rushing and breaking the old lock without much fight, but rather like a clean-cut boy next door.

She stands by the doorway and shakes her head.

"What're we gonna do with you, Ed? You know you ain't supposed to be fishing the Net for crotch fruit."

"You have no right to be in here," a weasely, snotty little voice says.

"Your roommate invited me in. Or is that your girl?"

Lainer doesn't say anything, trying to play it cool as he sits up and looks away from her.

"Bet she doesn't know you like the little ones," Barrick says, moving closer. "Don't worry, your secret's safe with me."

The face of the computer screen is finally visible as she nears the lanky guy.

"You wouldn't happen to be in one of them *private* chat rooms by chance?"

His eager hands wander over to try and log off and she moves in by his side.

"I'd keep your sweaty hands off that keyboard if I was you."

Lainer looks up at her, and contemplates continuing to try and log off.

"Trust me. You really don't wanna go there."

This time Lainer swallows, looking away from her, his hands and his body remaining immobile.

"I want to see my lawyer," Ed says to her.

There are a hundred reasons why Barrick doesn't want to be in this room with this waste of a life. Another hundred why she doesn't want to even look at his laptop much less touch it. But she knows the clock is ticking for little Mikayla. And no matter who and what her mother used to be, she's still gotta be worried sick.

"Why? Not even sure I'm gonna charge ya with anything yet. Though violatin' probation's gonna kick ya back to Parish Prison. As I recall, you didn't have such an easy go last time."

The dull, flat face just stares at her.

"The one thing they don't tolerate on the inside is child molesters."

She doesn't have to see the beads of sweat to sense them on Lainer. He looks like he's already in a world of hurt.

"What you wanna know?"

"You heard any chatter on there 'bout Mikayla Ames? Li'l black girl. Four years old. Photo's been in every paper. Not that I take you for a *Picayune* reader."

"There's been some ya-ya. But no one's owned up to it yet. Usually takes a month before the video hits the chat rooms. But I don't think there's too much of a demand for this one."

This one. Two words that put everything in a dark, lifeless context.

"Why's that?" Barrick asks.

"Little black girls are an acquired taste. Now white lambs or Asian cherubs, that's a whole other thing. Can't seem to get enough of those."

Barrick looks the room over again, then glares back at the man. She clamps her hand over his bony shoulder blade. "Keep an eye on those chat rooms. And don't think about going anywhere 'cuz I'll be back."

—21—

Kari lies down on the king-size bed that used to be her marital sacred space and refuge from the world. She feels used, abandoned, alone.

She looks at a bottle of Xanax that she took out of the bathroom. It waits for her.

The pills tempt her, but not enough.

She turns off the light and closes her eyes.

For a moment, she sees animated eyes in her mind. Hears the high-pitched giggle. Feels the arms around her neck and the lips on her cheek.

Mikayla is still close enough to touch in her dreams.

Now she's alone again.

Her little baby angel is somewhere, scared and alone too.

Hopefully still alive. Hopefully still alive and breathing and waiting for Momma to take her back home.

$-22-$

The streets look hazy and all the same. Yet it doesn't matter. It's better than remaining still in a lifeless bed in a lifeless house. It's better than watching the alarm clock to see that only five minutes have passed since the last time check. It's better than just thinking about the man who took her baby girl, but not doing a damned thing about it.

Now Kari sits behind the wheel of her Lexus, driving to find something, anything. A stack of flyers that had been brought over when everybody gathered earlier today sits on the passenger's side. She knows there's still more work that can be done. Maybe she'll get lucky. Or maybe God will finally smile down on her and shine a little light her way.

The fabric of the sweatpants she's wearing makes her itch. It's probably because she hasn't worn them for some time. Or maybe because she's got a nagging itch that won't go away. An itch that's more than skin-deep. It's in her heart and in her soul and she's gonna be scratching 'til kingdom finally does come.

The map of West Bank rests in the seat next to her as well, but she's not following any map. She's following her gut and her gut tells her to just drive.

Her gut tells her that every man might be the M. K. That every ugly, haunted, sinister face might be hiding a secret, might be hiding a very big four-year-old secret.

The men in this world only want one thing and that's all.

The sidewalks are full of men who could be monsters. They look

at her passing. They watch her. Because at this time of night, this time
of early morning, there's little good walking these streets. Good can
be found in locked homes and full beds. Good can be found dreaming pleasant dreams. These streets and sidewalks and strangers that
glance her way are images straight out of nightmares.

The building with the dimly lit beer sign urging you to come in.

The man who stands at the curb waiting.

The nondescript van that slowly drives around like an animal on
the prowl.

So many options. Too many options.

Kari knows she needs to get off these streets.

The streets have never been good to her.

Never.

—23—

The gate she drives up to is supposed to keep the monsters out, not people like herself. But in the last forty-eight hours, the world has been turned on its side like a toddler playing with a toy. She's just one of the balls being tossed around inside the plastic container, helpless and bouncing without any direction.

"Evening, ma'am," the security guard says in a friendly voice.

He sees the car she's driving. That earns the right to be called ma'am.

"I'm a friend of the Walkers'," she says.

"Do they know you're coming?"

"No, not exactly," she says. "But Tia—"

"Then I'll have to call." He picks up a phone in the small hut he's sitting in. "Your name?"

"Kari Ames."

A window slides shut as the guard phones Tia. Kari waits, trying to act calm and normal, trying not to overthink or overreact. Yet with each passing second, something else begins to bother her. She just knows that something's wrong. Not just with her daughter and David, but with everything. With this life she's built and cocooned herself in.

She feels cold even though it's humid outside and her window is still down. She taps the wheel, trying to stay calm.

The window opens again and the security guard looks back at her, this time in a glance that's .not as friendly. "Unfortunately, Mrs. Walker isn't available at the moment."

They both know that's not the case.

"Isn't available?" Kari doesn't know what else to say.

"Maybe you should give her a call in the morning."

She wants to say something, but there's nothing she can say to this man. She rolls up her window and shifts the Lexus in reverse. She steps off the gas when the lights of another car blind her for a moment as they come up behind her, blocking her way out.

"I'll raise the gate so you can circle out."

He says that as if she's just going to do exactly what she's been told. She nods at the man, who doesn't have the faintest idea of the hell she's going through. He couldn't understand and he doesn't have to.

Once the gate opens, she drives through it and then floors the accelerator. She can imagine the guard screaming and cursing and trying to tell her to come back. But what's he gonna do? Chase her down with his plastic water gun and his faux cop badge?

If a real cop needs to drag her ass out of here, so be it.

Kari drives down the lane and takes the third right, then drives to the end of the lane where the houses are no longer considered houses but rather mansions. Where they don't line up next to one another, but rather sit on their elegant and fat lot with an immaculate lawn and a swirling, smiling driveway in front of a multimillion-dollar structure.

The Ameses are well-off but this is beyond well. This is plump and swelling like a fat Christmas goose with all the trimmings.

For a moment she expects to be standing there for a long time, knocking and ringing the doorbell to no avail until security hauls her away. But she soon sees a stunned Tia standing there at the doorway in her robe.

"David told you, didn't he?" Kari demands.

Tia's eyes tell the whole story. It's the look that she's given to others, a look she's given when talking *about* others. But never to Kari. Never *about* Kari.

Her friend steps out into the dark night and closes the door behind her.

"I'm not the only one," Tia whispers. "Wayne, Arthur, Grace, Pam—and God knows who else. They're convinced your past is why Mikayla's missing."

Your past. The words echo in Kari's mind.

The two words that feel like a blade slicing her throat and her heart.

Tia continues. "But I don't believe that."

Kari nods, trying to deal with what all this means, trying to figure out what to say.

"But you know how *proper* Les is," Tia says. "He's such an asshole sometimes. That man's been trippin' since he heard about your history. I'm just waiting for him to settle down."

"Tia, I need you. . . . I can't do this alone. That's why I've been calling—I wanted to tell you myself. I've wanted to tell you for a long time."

"I planned on calling you back right after he left for his board meeting earlier," Tia says. "You got no idea what it's like dealing with Les when he's like this."

"What *he's* like? For Christ's sake, my daughter's missing. Mikayla could be dead. I've been driving around all night like a damn zombie."

Tia puts her hands on Kari's arms. "Kari, you just gotta give me a little time."

Kari shuffles from one foot to the other with her arms wrapped around her waist.

"Time for what?" she asks. "For Les to get used to your girlfriend being an ex–drug addict, a whore? Just remember, Tia, we've all got our secrets. Including your sadity husband."

"What's that supposed to mean?"

"*Especially* with the nurses."

Kari's words are a stab in Tia's heart. She's about to say something, but hears the footsteps of the security guard approaching. Kari hadn't even noticed the Chevy truck that had pulled up in front of the house.

"Mrs. Walker. Are you all right?"

"It's okay," Tia tells him. "Really, it's okay. Mrs. Ames is about to leave."

For a long second, Kari just looks at her friend. Then she gets in her car and drives back off into the night.

Back into a place where she's welcome.

—24—

Tia is shaking. She needs to reach out and grab something. In the shadows of the entryway, Les is waiting. Tia looks at him and knows that it's him that she needs to grab, right around his neck.

"So what did she have to say, coming here like that in the middle of the night?"

"Nothing you don't already know, including the fact that you're messing around with that skank nurse of yours."

"What, excuse me?"

"You heard me."

He rolls his eyes while he gives a look of complete annoyance. "If you believe Kari, I know you've lost your mind."

Tia tightens her robe. "I don't have to believe on Kari's word. On the contrary, my mind has never been clearer."

She walks past him at the bottom of the staircase and enters the dining room. She collapses into the chair at the head of the table.

Tia closes her eyes. "I feel so ashamed. I'm ashamed of both of us."

Les has followed her and says, "See—that woman has you acting all emotional over nothing."

"*That woman* is my best friend and I just turned my back on her when she needed me the most."

Tia wants to get in her car and find Kari.

"You don't need a friend like her," Les says.

"You don't know what I need."

She walks over, stopping inches away from his face. "Let me be clear. If you don't end whatever it is you've got going on, I'm gonna leave you and take every dime you have."

He sighs, shaking his head. "Kari's life is falling apart and she's trying to drag you down with her, spreading lies everywhere."

"You promised me that nothing was happening and I believed you."

"Then nothing should change."

"Don't play me. You think I've had no idea?" Tia curses. "I've had three different people tell me they suspected something, and none of them was Kari. Until tonight."

"She's filling your mind with lies. Kari's lied about everything."

"Les, you know she has tried to tell me the truth in the past. But I wasn't ready to hear it, too busy placating you—as usual."

Tia walks around him and heads into the kitchen.

"You're supposed to listen to me. I'm your husband."

She turns around and clenches her teeth for a second. Then she snarls, "If you don't stop messin' around, I'll be your worst nightmare."

−25−

She tries to escape the reality of Tia abandoning her at the worst possible time. Tia and David and all the rest of them. Doing exactly what she had feared. Showing exactly why she never told any of them.

Don't think about that now, she tells herself as she keeps herself busy.

Kari is driving around, stapling and taping flyers randomly, up and down streets.

With her heart racing and her mind wondering where to go next, Kari looks at the list of sexual predators with addresses listed. She knows that this is crazy, but then again she's lived and seen crazy and she's lived through it. One name and address feels right.

Maybe God will grant her one wish and she'll win the lottery.

Maybe this will be the right name and the right numbers.

The house is average and appears asleep just like the rest of the street and city.

Kari climbs out of her car, not sure what she's going to do, but at least knowing she's going to be doing *something.*

She walks to the side of the house, unseen in the thick gloom of this night. Every window she walks by is dark and blocked by shades or blinds. She tries out three before reaching a basement window. For a moment, she kneels and tries to look in. Then she takes out her cell phone and uses the light to try and see inside.

"Hey, what're you doing?"

She jerks her head up and spots the silhouette of a man holding something that looks a lot like a shotgun. He's standing at the edge of the house, then quickly begins running toward her as she begins to bolt away.

She expects a roar to tear through the night until her mind tells her that the man is carrying a baseball bat.

She sprints back to her car and climbs in it, ducking as she starts the car, expecting the bat to rip through her side window any second.

Kari drives for ten minutes before finally sitting upright and slowing down the car and breathing in and out.

What the hell are you doing? she says to herself.

The beating in her chest almost hurts. Just like her side. Just like her haggard breathing.

Just like her racing, chiming mind.

She manages to slow it all down, everything, even as she drives the car on autopilot, wondering what to do next and where to go.

−26−

There is only one place left to go. A place she's managed to avoid and run away from for the last ten years. But no longer.

The Jefferson Parish ghetto seems to say *Welcome back home* when she enters and finally parks her car.

The dizzy feeling in her head and her soul fling around like a jump rope swaying and turning and spinning. Her hands find her chest and they hold on to it, but she can't do anything. Something, someone, some kind of grip or vice is pushing against her. Beads of sweat dot her forehead and face and neck and arms. The trembling comes next.

Breathe damnit. Breathe, girl—get through this.

The end of a long night. The end of a very, very long night that started as a child and has been shadowing her ever since.

This is where it ends. In the place where so much of it began.

Once she slows down her breathing and the falling sensation fades away, Kari opens her eyes.

The dim light shows the local bar on the corner. She gets out of her car to go inside.

A local blues singer sings a song on a stage to the small crowd in the bar. She sits at the bar and orders a drink, something she hasn't done in years. She glances around the room and spots him.

The sweet, soft, satisfied feeling starts in her mouth the moment she takes the drink and warms down through her body and her soul. She can see the tall, lanky figure doing a deal with a young guy.

Everything in her tells her she needs to get out of here fast. But she doesn't.

She walks over to him knowing she looks out of place, but knowing the man won't care if she has cash.

"What'cha need, baby?" the hustler asks.

"What ya got?" she asks.

"Depends on how much is in that purse."

"I look like a chicken head to you? I done more dope than you got in all them baggy pockets."

The hustler gives her a look of surprise and cautiousness. Maybe he can see it on her face, not just the desperation and despair but the absolute deliriousness.

He knows enough not to mess with her.

"Chi gonna cost you ten."

"Chi?" she asks.

"Poor man's Oxycontin. A little H, some antihistamine, and a little a' Tylenol PM." He waits for her response, then asks, "Look, you buyin' or not?"

"Gimme two."

The twenty in her wallet gets her two vials. She grips them in a sweaty hand and then leaves the bar, leaving the figure to slink back into the shadows and soulful melodies of the bar.

Memories flood in. Strange hands on her, using her, beating her. Strange things she used to deal with those hands. Drugs and booze and whatever else could help her get by through the endless nights and the morning afters.

In an alley a few minutes later, with late night and early morning finally meeting up together in a silent dance, Kari parks the car and then studies the drugs.

Everything in her wants to escape.

Everything in her wants to stop what she *feels*. Even if it's just for a second.

Everything wants to just disappear.

She glances up at the rearview mirror, half expecting to see the hustler coming back toward her.

Instead, she sees the silhouettes of two figures arguing at the end of the alley. She can hear their voices, not able to make out what they're saying, but knowing they're yelling at each other.

A pimp with his prostitute.

She knows the sight well.

They're yelling and then she sees the man slap the woman in the face. Violently. Again, then one more time. She goes to her knees on the alley while Kari winces.

She closes her eyes, not able to take this.

She doesn't want to, but Kari remembers.

Memories that can come back in an instant . . .

$-27-$

*T*he leather in Lemont's car felt smooth and warm against her bare legs and arms. Her dress was tiny and tight and covered what needed to be. Kari waited for money she suddenly doubted might come.

"Get out of my face," Lemont said.

"I want what's comin' to me and you owe me—"

A slap across her face sent a violent surge through her whole body, an avalanche of ache.

"You want what's comin' to you, you stupid ho?" Lemont said, slapping her again and again.

Her face and body were numb. Her eyes were blinded momentarily, but her hand felt her leg and then inside the long high-heeled boot. She pulled out the blade and then shoved it forward just as he was about to strike her again.

Lemont's scream ripped through the car and the outside night just as she pulled open the door handle and stumbled onto the hard concrete street outside. Kari ran away from him, down a sidewalk and past an alley and then toward a church.

It was a small church she'd never noticed before. Kari hoped and prayed the door would be open. When she tried the handle, the door easily swung wide open.

Inside, the church was dark and silent. She was out of breath and sweating, her hand shaking as it still held the knife. She slid into the last pew in the church, then noticed the blood on her arms and legs. Some probably belonged to Lemont, while some was coming from the split lip that she could taste. She slowed down her breathing and wiped her legs with her free hand, then looked around.

She supposed the moon illuminated the stained glass window. Glancing outside, she could see Lemont dragging himself out of his car and heading to the church, but before he could make it, a police car stopped to question him. They spoke for a few moments, then Lemont went back to his car, glancing back at the church and seeming to think he'd better leave Kari to another day.

She lay on a pew, crying and calling out for Momma and Jesus, Lord.

−28−

K ari wakes up with a start. She'd fallen asleep when she closed her eyes against the sight of the man and woman in the alley. A sight that flashed her back to when she was with Lemont, when she was still on the street. Slowly, she opens her eyes and then glances back at the alley. As she stretches, trying to fully wake herself, she sees the vials on the dashboard where she left them. She rolls down the window and throws them out into the darkness and then drives away.

Endless secrets dwell in men's and women's souls. Unseen, unheard, and unwieldy.

Sometimes I thought I'd outrun that dirty girl who always
waited at the curb to be picked up with the rest of the week's trash,
but never did. Sometimes I thought I'd forgotten what
she looked like, that sad little soul of hers.

   If only I could go back and see her. To see her li'l smile.
   A smile like a green grassy field in the middle of the ghetto.
   Something so beautiful that just doesn't seem to belong.

ON THE THIRD DAY

− 1 −

Where have you been?" David demands.

She's not sure what to tell him. Kari's not sure herself where she went. Or more like *why* she went there.

"I was worried," he says, the tension easing a bit.

"I went out posting flyers and fell asleep in the car."

His face hardens again. "No more lies, Kari. Please."

"David, that's exactly what I did. I'm not in my right mind, but I'm telling the truth. Did Barrick or anybody call?" she asks.

"No—not a word from anyone."

"I cooked a little breakfast," David says. "Come on—why don't you have something to eat."

She shakes her head. "I'm not hungry. I need to take a shower and lie down."

She walks over to him.

"David, I'm sorry about everything. But right now we need each other's strength. I'm all messed up, I know—"

"Then please stop hiding things from me."

"Whatever you wanna know—I'll tell you. Are you ready for us to be finally honest with each other?"

His eyes explore her.

"I've always been honest," David says looking over her shoulder.

Then he breaks. A tear rolls from one eye.

Kari has never seen David cry. She goes to him and gently hugs him, tenderly kissing his face.

"Let it all out baby," she gently says to him.

He moves toward her.

The embrace is strong but also awkward. His muscles and touch feel tightly wound. Her feelings are a mix of relief and fear.

David moves closer and bends down to kiss her. And the knots unravel, the slightest bit.

For a moment, she loses herself in that kiss and his hands and the way he feels against her and on her.

David is behind her now, the edge of a kitchen counter in front of her, her eyes half-open, her heart wanting.

His lips suddenly feel rough against her neck and he stops.

"You should've never . . . let her out of your sight," he says in a half whisper.

The voice pops the bubble of passion.

"What?" she asks.

His hand grips her arm tight—too tight—and she can't help but wince.

"What are you doing?" her breathless voice says. "David, you're hurting me."

"I thought you'd be used to this," he says in her ear.

She jerks out from his embrace and turns around to face him, slapping him across the face before he can go any further.

"Think you can do me like that? Then ya better put money on the table."

His expression turns to shame.

"Zip up your pants 'fore I turn into who ya think I am."

Kari storms out of the kitchen and goes upstairs.

Instead of going in their bedroom, Kari enters her daughter's room and collapses on the bed. She weeps and finds Mikayla's blankie, clutching it the way her daughter might. Then she looks at the closet, remembering, knowing.

Soon the shadows in the room swallow her.

So does sleep.

It wraps itself around her skin and her soul and it opens her up to memories. To the familiar shadows of a childhood running around scared. To the dark, cloudy spaces in a small, confined hospital room.

— 2 —

The woman on the bed covered in tubes and holding her hand was someone she knew well.

"Remember," *the shaky voice began to tell the twelve-year-old.* "You can do anything you put your mind to, baby girl."

The words were like a drop of warm, dark chocolate on her tongue.

"I love you, Mommy."

She reached over and hugged her mother. The girl known as Mikayla embraced the woman known as Mommy.

She whispered in her ear.

"You and your daddy are gonna have to take care of each other."

Mommy squeezed her tight, then added, "Make me proud."

"I will," *she said.* "I promise."

The soft, gentle face that was bloated from those tubes and medicine but still beautiful—still always beautiful—smiled as shaking hands removed a cross from her neck and gave it to Mikayla.

"This is yours, Mikayla. . . ."

The dream wrapped itself back up in the blankets and the darkness of night. The sound of a door opening awoke her. Not Kari, but Mikayla.

She was in her bedroom. That bedroom. The bedroom belonging to the child.

No.

The shuffle of heavy feet, then the figure standing by her bed.

NO.

"You remind me so much of your momma," *the voice said.*

She shook. The voice didn't belong to her father. It was the sound of a man she didn't know. A man hungry and frustrated and needy.

"It's okay," *he said in a soft, sick voice.*

This dream was a nightmare. The monster had slinked into her room and found her. Her protector was no longer there.

Let me wake up, let me leave this place.

She tried to get up, but she couldn't.

I'm just a little girl, just a little angel. Why would anybody wanna hurt me?

The man, the figure, the monster held her down.

Nobody was in the room to help her or to hear her crying out.

Nobody was in this house that just belonged to the two of them.

"Your Momma told you to take care of me, baby girl," *the monster said in a sickening, hungry voice.* "You don't wanna let her down . . . not now when I need you."

She felt tears and reached out and tried to close her eyes and wish this away, but she couldn't.

She would forever be twelve years old.

She would forever be that frightened little girl.

— 3 —

She soon finds herself in the garage, searching through boxes. Against the wall, covered in dust and packing tape, is a box that she opens. It's notably smaller than the others.

Inside is the necklace her mother gave her. She hadn't thought of it for a long time.

She picks up the cross and holds it as if she's still dreaming. Her hand shakes.

The memories never really truly leave her. Never.

– 4 –

I've always been honest.

The words David said to Kari earlier now haunt him. As he sits in his parked car looking at old emails on his iPhone, he knows he has no right to demand honesty from his wife.

For a moment he thinks of Beth.

Don't do this, a voice inside tells him. *Don't go there.*

But he does.

A man can bury a secret, but that doesn't mean the secret goes away.

He searches through emails until he finds this one. There were many of them, but this was the first. And like many of those emails, David knows he should simply delete this and move on, just like he's managed to do with this backstory. But something in him can't delete this note.

It was sent after Beth had worked for him for a year.

I'm not sure whether I should write this and send it to you because I don't know what you'll say or do. I know I'm risking my job and my future at Tulane, but I left you this evening with a lot of unspoken words.

These are the words that were going through my mind.

I'm not a fool, David. And I'm not a child either.

There was something that happened tonight in the office. When I asked you what you were thinking, what you were *really* thinking, and when you brushed it off—I got angry because I don't want you to be coy. Not with me.

I don't operate that way.

This past year has been amazing. You have opened up my mind in so many ways. You've shown me that there can be more between a man and a woman than simply raw intensity and raw need. You've not only been my boss, David, but you've become one of my closest friends.

And yes, I've fallen. My heart and soul have both fallen.

I know what you were thinking tonight as we were talking and laughing. That look—the one before I asked you what you were thinking—there's only one thing you *could* be thinking, David.

I'm a big girl. And I know.

So this is me putting my cards on the table. All of them.

I'm yours if you want me. I know you have a family and I know you love them. And that's okay.

But I'm here if you need something else, something more. I'm not asking for your hand in marriage and not asking for anything more than what you want.

David—I know what you want. And this is me being totally honest with you.

I just want a little honesty back.

Beth

Even now, rereading this brings a certain excitement back to him. At the time, he could barely believe that Beth had sent this. They had been developing a relationship. Since adjusting to becoming parents, and then becoming buried at work, it had snuck up on him, this friendship with Beth.

She had finally told him everything, but even then, David had not been totally honest with himself.

It's just a small crush, he had told himself.

Yet he never thought of the need to get rid of Beth. Never. He had decided he would tell her that he was happily married and that she was a hard worker and that they could be friends but only friends.

Yet he never deleted this email nor told anybody else about it.

I know what you want, Beth had said in this email.

Two years later, David knows Beth was right. He had been trying to fool himself and everybody else. But he hadn't fooled Beth.

Eventually, he stopped fooling himself too.

— 5 —

Everybody knows that Barrick doesn't give up. Some call her persistent, others call her stubborn. But she's seen it all and been everywhere and it's that determination that's helped her manage day after day. Just like now.

She's been digging for some time. The names and the suspects seem to blur until the detective comes across a known pimp.

Barrick gets Frank's attention in the office with a "Well, well, well."

"What is it?" he asks.

"Here's a familiar name. Lemont Bullock. Looks like before he brought his business here, he was working out of Baton Rouge. He bailed Kari out of jail a couple of times."

Frank nods. "Okay, so she was in his stable."

"Looks that way to me."

Barrick rubs her eyes, tired from thinking and reading and searching and examining.

It's a possibility. And now anything that's a possibility is something.

6

The detective sits at her desk noticing the visitor. "Hi, Mrs. Ames."

"We got three days before Mikayla winds up dead like the others," Kari says without as much as a hello.

"Is that why you trespassed on private property at two in the mornin' last night?"

Kari stands there without anything to say, the fight and anger in her suddenly gone.

"Security got your license plate," Barrick continues.

This just deflates her even more.

The detective continues as if reading her mind. "Look—he wasn't your kidnapper. Piece a' shit moved out weeks ago. Megan's Law ain't always up-to-date."

Kari still refuses to acknowledge that she was even there. The detective might ask her other questions, ones that she doesn't want to answer.

"You know, you coulda got yourself shot. Everybody's on edge with folks thinkin' M. K.'s gonna grab their kids."

"I'll take that risk if it means finding Mikayla."

Barrick stands to look Kari square in the face. "Believe me, this department's usin' every resource available and then some. The mayor called in the big guns. Your family has some connections."

Good, Kari thinks as she nods. *At least some people are out there doing everything they can.*

Barrick glances at her watch. "Fact, FBI should be her any minute."

Those three letters—*FBI*—seems to be like a pill for Kari. The very mention of it gives her this burst of energy and hope. And any-thing—anything bright and hopeful and positive—is something.

Barrick walks over to her, moving a chair for her to sit in. When Kari's sitting, the detective asks her a question.

"Mrs. Ames, when was the last time you heard from Lemont Bull-ock? Would he have a reason to take your daughter?"

The name seems to slap her face just like Lemont used to do himself. She gives the detective a stern glance.

"It's been a while. I haven't been to Baton Rouge in years."

Barrick moves closer to her and leans against the desk. "Well, he moved here three years ago. I just thought I'd check it out."

Kari can't say a word. The thought has crossed her mind, but she doesn't think Lemont's the one. He wouldn't go to all the trouble abducting Mikayla. Plus, she's never told him about Mikayla, so she doubts he even knows they have a child.

Barrick seems to think for a moment. "He's the kinda guy who would have asked for money by now—if he had taken her. I know there's no ransom note, but I still wanna bring him in."

"He's too lazy to try to kidnap someone, especially a young girl."

"You sayin' he didn't do this?"

Kari shakes her head. "He liked to hurt women, but I don't think he has it in him to hurt a child."

"You'd be surprised by the things people have inside of them."

Kari's been paying Lemont on time regularly. Everything has been fine with him.

But what if . . ., a voice starts to ask.

Kari wants to change the subject. If Barrick discovers she's been paying Lemont, and then David finds out the truth . . .

She's quiet and doesn't know what to say until she notices a pic-ture on Barrick's desk.

"Is that your son?"

"Yes. He's fifteen and itchin' to drive. The boy's with his father most of the time."

Kari nods.

"I got the career. He got my son." Barrick smiles. "He sees me every other weekend . . . whether he likes it or not."

For the first time since this all happened, Kari feels like she can understand where this detective is coming from. There's a common bond shared. Any mother knows. They just know.

"Ah, there's our man from Baton Rouge," Barrick says as she stares out into the hallway, in the direction of the dark suit and flashy tie. When Kari focuses on his face, she gasps. The strong, square face of the African-American striding into the office takes her breath away.

"Mrs. Ames, meet Special Agent Wil Bennett."

He blinks his eyes as if something has flown in them.

"Mrs. Ames," Wil says, as a smile widens across his face.

"Mr. Bennett," Kari says in a tone of disbelief.

She forgets about the extended hand and instead wraps her arms around him in a hug. "You're the FBI agent? Well . . ." She doesn't really know what to say, seeing this face from her past. A welcome face this time.

"I'm so sorry about your daughter, Mikayla, Mrs. Ames. I'm gonna do everything I can to find her." Wil motions for Kari to sit again and pulls up a chair for himself. "How are you holding up?"

She nods. "Barely."

He's still the same. Still able to stare her down in a second. Still able to see behind her steel curtain of resolve and restraint. Wil is doing that right now, looking her over in disbelief.

"It's a small world," Barrick says.

"You told her?" Kari asks.

"I said we went to school together," Wil says, leaving it at that.

Kari knows this is all Wil would have said, leaving the other details of their relationship out of the picture. She doesn't want Barrick to know they were more than friends. The detective doesn't need to know that. It might just complicate matters even more. The same way telling her about Lemont would muddy up the already messy waters.

"I'd like to talk to David," Wil says.

"Of course."

"We don't have any leads just yet, but that doesn't mean anything. You just have to remain hopeful, okay?"

A phone call interrupts their conversation as Barrick answers it and then says she needs to excuse herself. Kari says she's just leaving, her business here finished now that she's seen Barrick doing everything she can.

Wil nods at her and says, "C'mon, I'll walk you out."

He walks beside her in an attentive manner.

"I wish this reunion was under better circumstances," he says to her as they reach the doors of the police station.

She nods. "I know. God must have sent you for a reason and I'm thankful for it."

"And believe me," he says with raised eyebrows, "the FBI has resources."

Kari gives a polite smile, but says nothing. Wil continues talking.

"So when Barrick sent me Mikayla's file with a family photo— let's just say I was surprised."

Wil studies her with an astonished look on his still ruggedly handsome face. She fights the urge to look away, hating to be examined too carefully.

"Nothing's changed," he tells her before she leaves.

7

The doorbell wakes him up out of his half-slumber. David is sitting there on the couch dressed in his suit and bow tie but unable to move. He rubs his eyes, then feels the scruff of beard he forgot to shave this morning. When he opens the door, the first thing he sees is the immense white orchid. Holding it in one arm, Beth stands on the porch with her other arm holding a stack of papers and mail.

"I brought those items you wanted from your office."

He can't help staring at the flower.

"It's from the humanities department," she says as he takes it. "Along with this card. Everybody wanted you and Kari to know you're in their prayers."

David nods.

"I'm sorry," Beth says. "You forgot I was coming by?"

"No, please, come in."

As he puts the plant down on a table, he adds, "I could use the company."

"Where's Kari?" Beth asks as she enters the doorway, her heels tapping on the hardwood floor.

"Not sure." David fights a yawn as he slowly breathes and tries to wake up his brain. "You want some iced tea?"

"Why not?"

David finds iced tea and pours her a glass. He watches her move, the skirt and shirt fitting her like glove. He goes over and gives her the drink as she sits on the couch.

"That unshaven look suits you," she says looking up at him.

"Trust me, it's not intentional. I can't seem to get myself together."

The face looking at him smiles. It's a warm and sweet smile, the kind that's comforting to see.

Even after everything that happened, David and Beth ended things on amicable terms. They both admitted that it had been a mistake, a mistake lasting over several intense and emotional months. They had tried and hoped to let things pass. And somehow, Beth had been true to her word. She could move on, as she had told him. She could be fine and not bring drama into his office and home.

"C'mon, David." She brushes back her long hair draped over her shoulder, then gently rubs her neck. "You'll find your daughter and you'll get through this."

He nods and smiles in a thankful manner. Then he unknots his bow tie and tosses it. He doesn't know what he was thinking putting it on in the first place.

"I appreciate you taking over my classes," he said. "I know it's more than you signed up for, but I have no doubt half my students prefer looking at you more than me."

Beth crosses one of her legs as she smiles and turns to face him. "No worries. You have to focus on your daughter."

He takes a sip of iced tea. "That's all I've been doing. And it's driving me crazy. Not knowing. All I can do is imagine. Imagine things I can't even bear to think about. I'm tired of thinking."

"I'm sure," Beth says.

"I can't turn my mind off. I can't do anything but wonder."

"You're going to be fine."

"I know I shouldn't be talking to you about this—it's just . . ."

Beth slides next to him and puts an arm around him. A soft, warm, caring arm that allows him to cry as long as he needs to.

"It's gonna be okay," the voice tells him. "I'm here for you, David. Whatever you need—I'm here."

— 8 —

Lemont would never call this place home, but it is the place he usually ends up to sleep and shower and shave. Unit six in the Iberville housing project probably never feels like a home to anybody, but at least it's a cheap place to stay. He looks forward to taking the money he's stacked up and moving out of this dump.

He doesn't know whether to believe this young body on the sofa beneath him or not. In his mind, she's good at one thing and one thing only. Otherwise, he thinks she has the sense of a horse and knows she has a taste for drugs.

"You sure ya ain't seen no envelope left for me?" he asks again.

"I swear, baby." He looks at her like the trash he thinks she is.

She puts her hands on one of his, but he's no fool.

He checks the mail flap in the door again, then opens it to check the dusty, dirty entryway.

"That's funny, 'cuz she ain't never missed a payment." He looks at the girl on the couch that's all arms, legs, and a thong. "You better not be lying."

Out of habit, he flexes his muscles. He's cut for knocking heads and tails around.

Lemont's going to make sure she doesn't know anything when he hears a knock on the door. He thinks maybe it's the person he's asking about, coming to bring her money late. When he opens it up, he sees someone else.

"Who are you?" he demands.

The tough, no-nonsense woman at the door with the cowboy hat flashes a badge at him. "Detective Gail Barrick. You must be Lemont."

He curses to himself as he just stands there, waiting to be cuffed or put down on the floor.

"When was the last time you saw Mikayla Carter?"

"Who?"

"Mikayla Carter—you remember her, right?"

He shakes his head. "I ain't seen that bitch in years."

The detective pushes him aside as she walks into the apartment and starts looking around.

"What's up with you?" Lemont shouts. "You got a warrant?"

The woman sees the naked woman, scrambling to get out of the room. "No. You got a license to sell young girls?"

Lemont stands by the door, waiting for her to get her business done and then leave him alone. But the detective is in no rush.

"I didn't know that bitch had a little girl. Hell . . . if she does, it could be mine!"

Barrick walks over to him, then grabs his neck and slams him against the wall. She squeezes her hand and grits her teeth. "Listen, you scumbag. You better just pray that nothing connects you to her daughter—'cuz I will put your ass away for good. You got that?"

She lets him go to cough and massage his neck, then leaves this dump. She's halfway down the hall when he yells out, "You think I'm scared of you? I ain't scared of no bitches. You hear me?"

Lemont pulls his head back in and slams the door. He grabs his keys.

"I got some business to take care of," he tells the still-cowering little thing as he leaves her and the apartment behind.

— 9 —

Kari drives in silence from the police department, still in shock from the sight of Wil. "Have mercy," she says to herself. It's one thing for there to be someone she knows and trusts on this case. But, this man . . .

She turns onto her street and sees the glow of candles lining her lawn, flickering in the darkness. There are people standing with candles in their hands, a vigil for her little girl. Streamed along the driveway is an assortment of flowers, teddy bears, and cards.

These aren't her friends, but rather ordinary good, decent people coming out to show them support and care.

She sees one of the search-team leaders and asks, "Are you guys still doing a nine thirty search at Crown Point?"

"Yes, ma'am."

"Give me a minute, I want to go with you."

As she starts to head inside, several reporters flank her.

"Now that the FBI is involved, do you feel more confident?" a blond-haired man asks her.

How do they know that? Kari wonders.

She stops and glares at him. "Who the hell told you that?"

"So it's true?" His white teeth seem to glow as he grins.

"Get off my property," she barks out.

This guy is as tall as she is and he seems to know that she would kick his ass all over this driveway and street. He backs out onto the sidewalk.

"Would you like to make a statement, Mrs. Ames?" another reporter asks her.

"No . . . , er, yes."

She knows she shouldn't, that she should go inside and see David and deal with him and what's next. Yet as the reporters circle around her with lights and mics and cameras, she collects herself and knows she has to do this.

She pictures her daughter's round, loving face with just a blink and a breath. "Please, whoever took Mikayla—my husband and I will do anything you ask to get her back. If it's money, name your price. Just return our daughter safely to us—please."

The lights and the cameras stare at her.

But like everything and everybody else, they have nothing to tell her.

$-10-$

In the darkness of a home dungeon, a young girl fights nightmares with the hope of prayer.

"Now I lay me down to sleep."

She feels her body shake and she pauses and waits for the shaking to stop.

"I pray the Lord my soul to keep."

She stops and thinks for a moment.

"God, please send Mommy and Daddy to come get me. I want to go home 'cuz this place is very scary. Amen."

A piece of me was missing, like the moon looking for its stars, like the sun looking for its horizon. Day turned into night and back into day. Yet the hurt inside only kept rising, kept comin', kept hurtin'.

That peace that passes all understanding—the kind they talk about—was like a flowing cool spring.

But I was standing barefoot and bare-souled in the middle of a barren desert.

Running and searching.

Running and searching in vain.

ON THE FOURTH DAY

E verything is different.
    The sound of the birds singing. The sparkle of the sun in the backyard. The taste of the coffee and the cinnamon bagel. The touch of the newspaper in his hands. The feeling of being in this kitchen, empty and alone.

Everything is different, new, overshadowed, and overwrought.

David tries to take in life at this moment, a step at trying to be productive. Yet even in his regular routine, the evil hovers all around him.

David gets through a few pages of the paper before he hears the quiet strides belonging to his wife. She walks to the coffeemaker and pours herself a cup.

"We searched the Rigolettes swamps all night long," he says, feeling an ache in his legs. "Thank God we didn't find her there."

"I was with the other team all night," Kari says, looking out the window.

The moon still hangs above, a faint glow in the morning sky.

"I spoke to Detective Barrick," David says, trying to start off the day on the right foot with Kari. "She said they were bringing in the FBI."

His wife just stares out the window in the morning sun. "Yes, I know. I met Wil when he came into the police station. In fact, I know him from Baton Rouge."

"Small world, huh?" he says.

"Yes, it is. God moves in mysterious ways."

"Someone from your past—this should be interesting."

"He's coming by later to discuss the case," Kari says as she goes to get herself some breakfast.

Soon she's sitting at the round breakfast table across from him. She begins to eat, but David is looking at her oddly, as if waiting on something. He doesn't have to say anything. She knows.

"When God shows up for Mikayla, I'll bless his damn food."

David shakes his head. "That's not how it works."

"You gonna tell me how it works now?"

He deliberately stops himself from saying something he regrets. But that doesn't stop Kari.

"When you gonna open your eyes? There's no reason for anything. God's just like Mikayla's blankie. Just 'cause it made her feel secure, doesn't mean it has any real power."

Once again, David remains silent.

"Know what today is?"

He can only nod.

"Why didn't you say something?"

"What do you want me to say? Put another candle on her birthday cake?"

Tears line Kari's cheeks, but he just sits there, saying nothing, doing nothing.

"What's happened to us?" Kari's weak voice seems to whisper.

"I don't know."

"How can just . . . everything suddenly . . . fall apart like this."

"Don't," David says.

"Don't what? Don't admit that Mikayla isn't the only thing that's suddenly gone missing."

"You should have told me about your past."

"So what? So you could suddenly act like another man who's horrified at his wife? He just cannot fathom his wife not being the angel he thought he married?"

"Don't give me that."

"I didn't tell you 'cause I knew you'd be like this."

"Is there anything else you're not telling me?"

"You still don't trust me? After all this?" She looks enraged. "At least I've always been here in this relationship."

"What's that supposed to mean?"

"You know *exactly* what it means. You and your precious career. I felt abandoned after Mikayla was born."

"You admitted that you were suffering from postpartum depression," David says.

"So that gave you the right to disappear?"

"I didn't disappear."

"Sometimes I thought—after having Mikayla—that you didn't want me, that you didn't want us."

"Stop it."

"Sometimes I've thought other things—I've wondered . . ."

"I'm not going to have this conversation now about us when Mikayla's out there."

He stands, leaves his coffee cup in the sink, then walks out.

David doesn't want to hear what Kari's thought about and wondered. Because he fears she might suspect something happened between him and Beth.

I can't deal with that now, he thinks. *That's in the past and it needs to stay in the past until we deal with this present nightmare.*

– 2 –

The bottle of vodka is easy to find.

Kari unscrews the top of the bottle without feeling guilt or shame or remorse. She takes a sniff. The sweet smell of yesterday rises to her nose.

She pulls out a glass. Her hand and her body and her soul have gone numb. She doesn't want to drink to take away the pain. She wants to drink to feel something. Since every bad thing happening— this helpless, hopeless rotting feeling—seems to be all her fault.

She takes a sip and doesn't flinch and doesn't blink. It slides down easily.

Then she takes another.

— 3 —

The glow of the computer screen is like the warm face of a fire to CSI Officer Frank Donovan. He spends a lot of his time staring into it, typing away, waiting for results. He's used to typing and watching and waiting. It's part of the job. The more time goes by, the more advanced his work becomes and the more sophisticated technology gets to help them catch killers and creeps.

It's the middle of the day and Frank is running a new bit of software that he recently installed. It's shoe-recognition software that is able to match the sole of the shoe to a brand. In this particular case, the one with the missing Ames girl, he's looking to match the boot print found at the base of the window near the house. It goes through a hundred different names: Timberland, Carhartt, Red Wing, Caterpillar.

It's amazing how quickly the software works.

The results show on screen in no time. He sees the boot type.

Blundstones.

He prints out the search results and goes to give them to Detective Barrick.

It's a huge jigsaw puzzle with so many pieces missing. Maybe this one will make the difference.

— 4 —

Barrick is watching Wil on the computer as he's prowling around on the Internet in chat rooms. She looks to find his name is BETSY11.

It's not the ones we already know about who worry me, the detective's told others before. *It's the ones we don't have the faintest clue about, the ones who smile and live their lives and secretly take the very thing that's not ever supposed to be taken.*

"So what's up, Betsy?" she asks the FBI man. "Seems you're already in a chat room."

Wil sends an instant message to someone named LIKEM-YOUNG.

"This creep—LIKEMYOUNG—thinks Ed Lainer already got rid of her."

Wil types away and glances at the screen while Barrick watches.

"There's nothin' like a common bond to build a trustin' relationship. Though I am startin' to get worried about ya."

The handsome face glances back at her, curious. "Why's that?"

"You're way too comfortable playin' a prepubescent girl."

"One of the hazards of the job."

She studies the monitor. "Send LIKEMYOUNG a photo yet?"

Wil shakes his head. "Naw—I don't want to scare him away by coming on too strong. Gotta let wacko come to me."

"These pedos ever get to ya?"

"All the time." He just stares into the monitor, his square jaw solid, his gaze lost in some other place. "When you've seen what I've seen, you don't even know if you should have kids."

Barrick reads LIKEMYOUNG's newest instant message. "He ain't sure about a hookup?"

"Likes 'em younger. And black."

"Ask how young," Barrick asks. "Maybe he's got a lead on Mikayla."

Wil types the question and then they wait on the answer.

"I'll tell you when I see you," Wil reads.

Barrick keeps reading the perverse text. "Now he wants to bring along a friend?"

"The more scumbags the merrier."

"This fella's pretty cagey. Must've seen too many *Dateline NBC* specials."

"Man's sexual drive is a powerful motivator, even when common sense should prevail."

They wait for another response.

"He took the bait," Barrick finally shouts out.

It might be one step closer to Mikayla.

Hopefully alive, the detective thinks.

– 5 –

L ord, where are you?"
David sits in his car, knowing this is no refuge or sanctuary, yet also not knowing where else to go.

He's been at the police station twice today. Neither time has he been able to find the FBI agent that Kari knows. Neither time has anybody given him any more answers about Mikayla. Yet both times, valuable time has leaked out like birdseed being eaten away and scattered all over the ground.

He feels like a tiny seed lost in the mulch. Unseen and unheard.

"God, help us please."

He went to the university, but proved to be utterly useless there. Seeing Beth only reminded him of his deep-rooted fears and shame. Today she wasn't a comfort. She was a mirror of regret and remorse.

David sits here and knows he needs to go back home, yet he fears what he's going to find there. A woman he no longer knows and trusts. A mother out of her mind with grief and fear. Normally David would be standing beside her with his arm clasped tightly around her, telling her that they would get through this, that they would be okay. But he had just learned that there was really no *we* to begin with.

Kari's left a few voicemails on his phone. He looks at his emails in his parking space at the university. Then he tries to waste some time by going on Twitter. Bored yet desperate for answers is a bad place to be.

A tweet from their pastor is seen near the top of his phone.

God is ur everything! He's ur joy in the time of sorrow. He's ur peace
in the time of confusion. He's ur power in the moment of weakness.

David reads this several times and he knows Bishop Jakes is right.

Yes, God is our everything. And yes, He should be our joy and our
peace and our power.

"This is our daughter," David says. "This is our *only* daughter,
Lord."

Then David stares out the window and realizes what he just said.

He remembers the Bible verse that's spoken to so many in trouble
times like this.

For God so loved the world that He gave His . . .

"Only son," David says.

Tears roll down his face.

He's not God and can't claim to know what God wants or needs.
All he can do is trust and pray. Trust and obey. Trust and hope.

David starts the car and knows he needs to be home to be with
Kari.

— 6 —

Later in the evening, as Wil knocks on their door and then steps in the entryway of the Ames house, he notices a garbage bag near the front door needing to be taken out. Papers and more papers strewn about everywhere. Shoes and clothes on the floor.

Kari appears to have just woken up. "Excuse me, Wil. And excuse the house. I was up all night with a search party."

"It's fine—I understand," Wil says.

"Sorry about the mess," she tells him as she tries to clean up a bit. "I used to be a clean freak. But ever since Mikayla . . ."

He just nods, not saying anything. He feels like he's disturbing their privacy even though they had planned on him coming by.

Kari then seems to realize the time. "Are you hungry?" she asks, wringing her hands and turning in her tracks as if trying to get her bearings.

"No, but if I'm intruding, I can come another time—"

"Please, no. Stay. I'm going to warm up food some folks brought over."

Wil watches as she takes the covering of tinfoil off the glass dish. Despite the situation and the years apart, he can't help taking her in. Kari is still beautiful. He wishes the circumstances were different. He has so many questions that don't have to do with her missing daughter. Questions that he can't even begin to unravel, not now, at this point in her life.

The sound of footsteps comes behind them. Kari pauses in her movement. "Wil, this is my husband, David."

Wil nods. She turns her attention to the dish and says, "Why don't you go in the living room and make yourself comfortable, Wil," Kari says. "It'll just take me a few minutes to get this ready."

Wil enters the living room and notices the stack of flyers on the coffee table. He passes a large white orchid.

"Nice orchid," he says.

"It's supposed to give us *strength*," David says.

Wil nods. "I'm sure you could use a lot of that right now."

David just continues looking at the orchid. Wil wonders about this guy, the husband. He knows that this man's only child has been missing for several days and gives him the benefit of the doubt. David, just like Kari, is doing everything he can just to remain sane. Just to remain standing.

Just as he's about to reach out and say something else to encourage this man, David wanders off down the hall, leaving him in silence.

This beautiful house feels very quiet. And very empty.

7

A few moments later, the couple and the FBI agent sit down for a dinner filled with awkward silences. Wil waits until Kari or David bring up Mikayla. Turns out it's David.

"What can you tell us about these cases, Wil?"

"In most cases, the victim doesn't know the suspect," Wil says as he finishes his plate. "But usually, there's been some kinda prior contact. M. K. probably observed Mikayla somewhere."

"Like where?" Kari asks.

"Anywhere the molester would have blended in—at the park, a public gathering, church even."

The words aren't comforting even if they're honest. Kari glances at David, who's barely touched his meal and has watched her like a hawk for the last half hour.

"In thirty-three percent of cases, contact between the abductor and victim takes place less than two hundred feet from home."

"So, Kari says you two know each other from Baton Rouge," David asks.

His question isn't as much for Wil as it is for Kari.

"Yes, we went to high school together."

Kari raises her eyebrows and smiles at their guest. "I was Wil's first love."

Wil chuckles at the thought. "I was fourteen. We were kids having fun. Anyway, I went off to college and we ended up losing track of each other."

David holds up his glass. "Here's to reunions."

Kari gives him a hard look.

"Oh, I forgot," David says to her. "You don't drink."

She grits her teeth and raises her glass, still refusing to lift her gaze off of his.

"They say it's bad luck to toast with water," David says. "But how much worse could our luck get, right?"

"Stop it, David," Kari says in a loud whisper.

He finishes his drink and Kari knows that she needs a real one. She stands up and gets her plate, bringing it in to the kitchen and dropping it with a loud crash into the sink. She finds the vodka again and downs another shot, not caring if David or Wil see her doing so. She's been drinking on and off all day and she's not about to stop. Not now.

— 8 —

So I hear you teach at Tulane," Wil says, making note of the crash of dishes in the sink, but remaining casual.

"Teach?" David feels his shirt around his neck tighten a bit. "I'm dean of the humanities department. I have a doctorate, Mr. Bennett. I publish and I lecture."

The FBI agent's face covers in a shadow of anger, but he doesn't say anything. Wil raises an eyebrow. He waits for David to utter the next words.

"I'm sorry—I'm not myself," David says.

"I understand."

"Really? Because all I can think about is what some bastard might be doing to Mikayla right now. To my daughter."

David feels like cracking the glass in his hand. He shakes his head, looking into the eyes of the man across from him. "And I can't do crap about it—and apparently, neither can you."

Just as it appears that Wil is about to say something, Kari strolls through the entryway to the dining room holding the birthday cake. A birthday cake with Mikayla's name on it. She had all day to work on it, especially while David was MIA.

"What is wrong with you?"

She's got a strange smile on her face, distant and smug and scary. David doesn't recognize the smile or his wife or what in God's name she's doing. She ignores him and puts the cake in the middle of the table, then starts to light the candles.

"Are you sick?" he yells and grabs her hands. Then it dawns on him. "You're drinkin' again?"

She pulls away from him.

"What's next?" David blurts out. "Crack? Turnin' tricks?"

She smiles and then slowly picks up his wine glass and brings it to her full lips. She finishes the glass, then licks her lips, smiling at him.

"Like you said: *Here's to reunions.*"

He picks up the nearest thing he sees—the pink cake with Mikayla's name on top of it—and hurls it against the wall. It doesn't explode, but rather clumps down into the corner in a soggy, frosted mess.

His body shakes with the force of a raging anger.

"I can't be here anymore," David says, starting to leave.

"You been looking for an excuse anyway. Now you got one. I'm tired of you judgin' me and actin' like I'm a guest in my own house."

David stops and looks for Wil's reaction.

"You don't even wanna try to understand me," Kari shouts out. "'Cause you already know everything. Right, *professor?*"

David has seen enough. He exits the house and leaves Kari and Wil alone.

— 9 —

Kari excuses herself to the kitchen, feeling sicker than ever. Wil waits, staying where he is for a few minutes, feeling sad for this tortured couple. He approaches the kitchen carefully, sticks his head in, and says, "Maybe I should go."

Kari shakes her head. "I'm so sorry. David and I have lost our minds over this thing. Please don't go just yet. Unless you just have to."

"Last thing I want is to cause trouble with your husband. I'm supposed to be here to help."

"You didn't cause anything," she says.

She's about to sit down when a knock at the door startles her.

"What's wrong?" Wil asks.

"Every time someone knocks, I think they're coming to tell me my daughter's dead."

"Then let me answer."

"No, I can do this," she says.

Kari heads to the door. The grinning face on the other side of it is possibly the last one she ever expects to see.

"What're you doing here?" she whispers to Lemont, as she steps into the door frame to have privacy.

"I warned you 'bout not sendin' my money."

"What? I slid the envelope under the door like I always do."

"Well, you musta not slid it good enough, 'cuz I ain't got it."

"Maybe somebody stole it."

She looks back inside to see where Wil might be, hoping he doesn't approach the door.

"Maybe you just better give me another envelope. Bitch, you causin' me all kinds of trouble. Cops showed up at my house—about your little girl."

"Did you take her 'cuz you couldn't find the money?"

"Hell no—I ain't into child snatchin'—and you better tell them to stay off of me."

She tries to close the door, but bony fingers grip around the edges and push against the door and her. Kari is slammed back to the floor. Lemont walks into the foyer and looks around.

"Well, I'll be," he says. "If I'd known ya was livin' this large, I woulda asked for more every month."

Wil is already behind her, staring at this scene. "Kari, what's going on here?"

"You need to leave, Lemont," Kari says.

Lemont sees the agent, knows it's not the husband, and backs up. But he doesn't go far. Wil yanks Lemont by his collar, pulls him back into the house. He lands on his back and head. Lemont quickly leaps back up and lunges at Wil.

Blood splatters on the floor and across Wil's fist.

"Wil, stop," she screams. "That's enough."

Wil picks Lemont up and leads him to the front door, opening it to bring him outside.

"I ain't through with you, bitch," a bloodied mouth screams at her.

"Come back again, I'll kill ya," Wil tells Lemont before closing the door.

With the door shut and locked, Wil just stares at Kari a moment, then puts his arms around her. "Now, tell me what that was about."

—10—

Kari watches him wrap up his cleaned hand with a damp towel to stop the bleeding.

"How long's he been blackmailin' you?" Wil asks.

"About a year and a half."

If only I'd known earlier, he can't help thinking.

"He spotted me downtown and I've been paying him to keep his mouth shut ever since," Kari continues.

"How'd you keep it from David?"

"The money came out of my account from selling real estate."

Wil nods and glances down at his hand. He knows he temporarily lost it, something he's not proud of. As he looks at Kari, he realizes that there are many things she needs. Many things he wants to give her.

"I better go," he says.

She looks back at him with scared, young eyes. "Just stay until David comes back. I don't wanna be here alone."

He understands.

Wil won't leave her alone. Not tonight. Not like this.

−11−

David doesn't know what he will find or what he expects when he pulls up to Beth's house. It's not the first time he's stopped here during the night. The house is dark and he wonders if she is still awake. He knocks gently, waiting until the light comes on.

The door cracks open, the chain lock is still on.

"David?" Beth asks in complete surprise. "What are you doing here?"

Good question.

"I don't know. I just wanted to . . . talk."

"Wow," her voice says, unusually nervous. "You know I'd like to be there for you. But now isn't a good time."

"Of course," he says, feeling foolish standing on her porch. "I understand."

"You sure?"

"Positive. Have a good night."

As David heads back to the dark emptiness of his car, he hears the door quietly shut behind him.

$-12-$

Kari assumes the phone call is from David when she picks it up. "Hello?" A pause and then nothing. "Hello?"

The silence fills her with fear.

Then she finally hears something. A faint breathing.

"Who is this?"

The breathing is heavy and deliberate, as if it wants to be heard. As if it wants to feel like it's breathing down her neck, against her ear, breathing through a half-opened mouth curled into a devilish smile.

"Please, if you have my daughter—"

Then the breather is gone, the line dead.

She puts a hand against her chest and can feel the beating. Then she slips on a robe and heads down to the kitchen.

Sleep is impossible. So is peace of mind. She just needs a little help. A little something.

In the kitchen, she finds help in a bottle and a full glass. She downs it with one swallow, putting the glass down just as she turns to see Wil.

"I couldn't sleep," she says. "The phone rang. I heard breathing, but no one said anything. . . ."

Wil looks serious, staring at her for a moment before saying, "Let me check the phone tap."

As he's gone to check the phone, Kari eyes the Hennessy. Before she can pour herself another shot, Wil walks back into the kitchen, heading straight for the bottle. He picks it up and pours it into the sink.

"Come on—let's go talk on the couch," Wil says as he guides her into the family room.

Kari sits and suddenly feels naked and exposed. It has nothing to do with what she's wearing, but more because of what she realizes this man sitting next to her knows.

"It hasn't always been like this," she tells him in a weak voice. "Things were working out for us—for David and Mikayla and me."

Wil nods.

"I'm not the same person who left you—who left Baton Rouge. So many good things have happened. I just wish—I wish you could have seen the good things. The best thing being Mikayla."

"You don't have to try and be anybody else to me," Wil says. "I knew who you were and it didn't change how I felt about you a bit."

"David's a good man," she says, suddenly feeling the need to defend him. "It's just—everything that's happened."

"I understand."

"I haven't had a drink in years. I've been clean and sober and things have been good. Life has been fine."

"Kari, you can't keep stuffin' life down. At some point, Mikayla Carter is gonna have to deal with what her father did to her. And changin' your name, marryin' a professor, and livin' in this big-ass house won't heal the hurt."

The words scold, but also speak the truth.

Hearing her name, and knowing that Wil knows about her father . . . Hearing him say the obvious, about her name and about David and about this home . . .

The tears are already streaming down her cheeks before she realizes they are there. She finds herself being held by Wil and his strong arms.

"There's nothing you're going to find in that bottle in the kitchen," Wil says.

"Yeah, but for the moment, it soothes my pain," she says about the liquor. "Wil—I don't know who I am anymore."

"Then let me remind you. You're a strong woman with a good heart."

She pulls away from his hold.

"I can't bear to think about what could be happening with Mikayla."

Wil moves closer to her again, speaking directly at her and making sure she's watching him. "You have to focus your energy on finding her. Don't let anybody or anything take away your strength. Do you understand?"

His eyes offer hope. His words offer comfort.

And once again, his arms offer sanctuary.

The fear of not knowing is the worst. It gnaws on your heart and soul, every moment of every passing day.

Silence only makes the mind scream out in anger and frustration. Ignorance only makes the mind paint scenario after scenario, each one worse than the last.

Impatience makes the uncertainty feel almost worse than knowing, one way or the other.

ON THE FIFTH DAY

– 1 –

David stands outside on the lawn, facing the street. Kari can see him from their bedroom window, just standing with his mug of coffee.

As if on cue, a flock of birds scatter from the telephone pole David is watching.

They fly in all directions, just like all the places that Mikayla could have disappeared to and all the leads they might be forced to follow up with.

Soon the sky is empty and the telephone pole is bare.

The man facing them looks that way too.

— 2 —

Kari is soon downstairs carrying a cup of coffee for their unlikely overnight guest. Before handing it to Wil, she sees David slip inside and head up the stairs.

"How'd you sleep?" she asks as she gives Wil the mug.

"That couch is more comfortable than I thought."

Wil takes a sip, but appears to be thinking of something else. Something is bothering him.

"I keep asking myself why six days?" he says. "Why wait to kill his victims? There is meaning in everything, even in its absence."

"Maybe it's an act of defiance against God's Sixth Commandment."

"Thou shalt not murder."

Kari nods.

"Maybe," he continues. "Let me show you something."

They head into the family room where all the information and details are still taped and spread out. He motions to a photo of the boots that's taped to the wall.

"M. K. was wearing Blundstones when he abducted Mikayla. Twenty-seven thousand pairs were sold in the area over the past three years. Mikayla was also the only abduction that occurred *inside* a house. All the others were yanked off the street."

"What does that mean?"

"Either M. K. was getting more bold or more desperate," Wil says. "It was nine weeks between Mikayla and his last victim."

"Which is the shortest time M. K. ever waited," Kari says.

"Right. It just doesn't fit his MO. Listen, Barrick's chasing down a chat-room lead—waiting for a meet up. C'mon—take a ride with me."

— 3 —

Through an upstairs window, David watches them getting into the FBI agent's car and driving away. Kari had said that Wil had an idea and that they were going to follow it, then she asked him if he wanted to go. Yet he had refused. Without even thinking about it.

Had it been out of stubbornness? Out of anger at Kari? Out of jealousy from Mr. Charming from the past suddenly showing up on their doorstep?

Perhaps it's all of those things and more.

David knows he should be in that car with them, going to wherever the investigation might take them.

Instead, David feels imprisoned. Not just in this house, but in his skin.

— 4 —

When Wil's car reaches the start of the long bridge, Kari knows for sure that they're not heading to the police station.

"Where are you taking me?" she asks, knowing that the Bonnet Carré Spillway heads out of the city.

She guesses that he's not attempting to run away with her. Not this time.

"I think it's time you paid someone a visit," Wil says, his eyes hidden behind his sunglasses.

"Who?"

"Just wait and see."

For a while, the water surrounding them begins to lull her to sleep. It's nice to be somewhere and just have a quiet moment.

Soon, Wil breaks the silence.

"I can't believe how you've changed."

She smiles. "My parole officer gave me two choices—jail or community service with a church."

"Of course you did the community service."

"They kept telling me over and over again, 'Let God take care of you. Let God take care of you.' I figured what did I have to lose at that point? I started praying, and somehow my entire life turned around."

"I'm proud of you," he says.

These four words mean more to Kari than any four words have meant for a long time.

She opens her purse and removes a photo, giving it to Wil. He takes off his sunglasses, then for a moment studies the picture in disbelief.

"Is that from prom night?"

"You know it is. I found it last night."

"Look at that dress," he says with a big grin. "You were styling."

She raises her eyebrows. "Don't start. Or I'll pop off about your sporting that high-top fade."

He glances at her and she remembers. His look and affection haven't changed.

"You always did have rose-colored glasses when it came to me," Kari says. "I haven't changed all that much—I'd only break your heart again."

"I'm stronger than you think. Besides, this time, I've got my eyes wide open."

Kari looks at the building in front of them. "I haven't been back here since I left Baton Rouge."

"Just go on inside," Wil says. "Anne's gonna drive you home and I'll call you later."

She nods and smiles, noticing he's not planning to give the picture back to her. As she says good-bye and exits the car, she tries to steady her emotions.

You can get through this just like you've gotten through everything before, Kari tells herself. *Just take deep breaths and slow down and relax. Everything's going to be fine.*

— 5 —

They are in a large room, twenty women of various ages, sitting on chairs in a circle. It looks like it could be an AA meeting, but Kari knows different. The woman speaking to the rest of the group is around fifty years old, loud and humorous, wearing clothes that don't match and look about as old as she is. Anne was the one who reached out to Kari years ago when she first showed up to a group like this, when Kari felt like nobody in this world would ever reach out to help her messed-up soul.

Kari still loves Anne. She watches and listens to the woman by the doorway.

"Aunt Phyllis never forgave me. She couldn't even understand why I'd told. Then, she concluded that her good husband wouldn't have screwed a ten-year-old girl unless I'd seduced him—because that's what kids do, right?" She pauses for a moment as she sees the newcomer. "Kari, come on in. There's an empty chair."

"I'm good," she says as she steps into the room, but still remains standing near the back wall.

"Like most kids, I tried to put it behind me and moved on with my life," Anne continues. "What nobody knows is—even today—the only way I'm comfortable is if I can control everything. And I mean *everything*. Unfortunately, the world rarely cooperates."

Kari eventually takes the empty seat and sits down. These are adult survivors of child abuse. Anne nods and smiles in her direction.

Anne is the closest thing Kari has to a living relative. She's the aunt she always wanted to have.

In a weird way, Kari feels like she's come home.

— 6 —

"City Park? That's only the largest friggin' park in New Orleans?" Wil is driving back to the station and talking to Detective Barrick on his cell. He doesn't like the news he's getting.

"I'll have teams at Wisner Boulevard, Harrison Avenue, and Marconi Drive."

"What about the decoy?" he asks.

"Our Betsy's fourteen, but looks eleven."

"This is day five."

"I know. That's why we need to cuff and stuff this pedo before we have another dead girl on our hands."

"Set it up," Wil says. "I'm on my way."

"By the way," Barrick adds. "We checked everything out on Kari's old pimp, Lemont. He's clean."

He laughs. "A clean dirtbag. Now that's a good joke."

— 7 —

When the ASCA meeting ends, it doesn't take long for Anne to walk over to Kari and give her a big hug.

"Girl, look at you."

"Never thought I'd be here again," she says.

"Will told me what's going on with your baby."

She nods and leaves it at that.

"I'm sorry I didn't stay in touch with you, Anne."

"All that matters is you're back," she says.

"Did Wil tell you anything else, about what's happening at home, about . . . anything else?"

The rest of the women file out of the room.

"I know you been drinking."

"I mean—the only reason I started was because of Mikayla."

"Don't blame your daughter," Anne says, reaching over to touch Kari's hand. "I know you. And we both know where this is coming from."

Kari shifts in her seat.

"Don't yield to the temptation to feel sorry for yourself," Anne chides. "This is a terrible thing happening to you. Terrible things have been happening to you for a long time. No doubt. But you've already been told, if you learn to forgive your father, the gates might open up. And, one day, you're gonna have to confront him."

"Why?"

"So you can forgive him. And yourself."

That is asking the impossible.

"I don't want to forgive him. Besides, the son of a bitch is dead."

Anne raises her eyebrows, the wrinkles around her eyes seeming to grin in delight. "You sure? 'Cause he still seems alive to me."

Kari rises from her chair and begins to start walking toward the door.

"Your relapsing and acting all crazy is *not* going to bring your daughter home! There'll come a point when you need to ask yourself if you have the courage to heal. It doesn't matter how you do it either. Some people write a letter they never send. Others scream at a wall. What's important is to get it out. All of it. That's the only way you'll ever start to feel again."

"I don't know . . . ," Kari replies, having stopped her movement out the door.

"You don't have to know right now," Anne says. "Do it when you're ready."

"Right now, all I can think about is finding my daughter."

Anne walks between Kari and the door, forcing Kari to look at her and listen.

"Nothing happens by chance. God's gonna see you through this. If you listen, you'll hear him talking to you now. Don't lose your faith now."

She feels the welling of tears in her eyes. "I'm trying not to."

"Not enough," Anne says shaking her head and waving her finger. "You've got to be stronger. If ever there was a time to pick yourself up, it's now. Whenever you get an urge just call me."

Kari nods, knowing that she has an urge this very moment.

I just gotta remember Anne's words, she thinks. *I gotta somehow, in some way, take them to heart.*

8

Wil watches Barrick move a chess piece on the board and wonders briefly if the detective knows how to play the game. Not that they're actually playing. He never learned, but it doesn't matter anyway. They're stalling and buying time. They sit at a picnic table in the middle of the busy Carousel Gardens. Families walk by. Mothers with strollers. Children running. There's a long line for the miniature train and another for the antique carousel.

Come on, Wil thinks as his eyes wander quickly without being obvious.

He knows that they're not the only cops around the area.

One cop is walking a poodle close to Wisner Boulevard.

Another cop is standing by Harrison Avenue, doing what he probably would be doing anyway: having a cigarette and relaxing.

Nearby on Marconi Drive, a third undercover cop is buying a corn dog from a street vendor.

They all circle around Betsy, their young and innocent decoy. The girl is fourteen years old and sharp as a tack, but she appears much younger. Betsy sits on a park bench alone, just another pretty little face in this pretty little park.

"It's almost four thirty," Barrick says softly. "Maybe LIKEM-YOUNG ain't gonna show."

Wil glances at her. "He'll show. He's just being cautious."

"Hopefully he didn't forget to bring the right socks." The detective looks at him and waits. "Your move."

He smiles. "I don't know how to play."

"Should've said so, sugar—I would've brought checkers."

"Funny."

"Just move one of your pawns."

As he does, a man around forty-something wearing a video camera slung around his neck takes a seat on a bench facing Betsy.

"Check out the tourist at six o'clock," Wil says, watching a Cajun man.

After a couple of minutes, the man bends down to tie his shoes.

"Damn," Barrick says. "He has black socks."

Wil absently moves another pawn even though it isn't his turn. His eyes carefully survey the area, looking for any possible suspect. Then he goes back to the stranger with the black socks.

Then he sees the man smiling back at Betsy.

The man smiles and then . . .

Rolls down one of his socks to reveal a red one underneath.

"That's him," Wil says.

Barrick grabs the radio that's hidden under the table and calls it in. "All units, we have a visual on the suspect."

The cops soon all begin to close in on Betsy and the suspect. He's starting to walk toward her, then he stops as he notices Wil coming his way.

The man drops his video camera and begins to sprint for the grass. Wil takes off after him, thankful that he stays in good shape, knowing the guy doesn't have a chance. You just never know when you're going to have to do a hundred-yard sprint after some scumbag.

Wil soon catches the man and slams him to the ground. In seconds the man's hands are cuffed behind his back.

"Where's your friend?" Wil shouts as he tries to catch his breath.

"I got no idea what you're talking about!"

Wil looks around and tries to see anyone who looks suspicious. Anybody.

But there's nobody around. Not a soul.

Just this little weasel.

I'll get it out of you, Wil thinks. *You're gonna tell me everything you know.*

9

His name is Martin Picou.

And Martin continues to play the innocent.

"Somebody hacked my email. You can't prove nothin', po-po."

Wil leans back in the chair next to Barrick. They've been in this small interrogation room for half an hour now. Beads of sweat dot Picou's forehead. He stinks of body odor and fear.

"Did that somebody also tell you to put on *two* different colored socks??"

This seems to shut up the lowlife.

"We already got you for solicitin' a minor," Detective Barrick says. "You might wanna start talking."

Martin's accent is thick. So is his arrogance. "If I tell you what you wanna know—I walk."

"Depends on what you give," Wil says.

Barrick taps the file folder on the table they're sitting at. "Checked you out, Marty. You into *beaucoup* shit."

"But li'l black girls ain't one of 'em."

Martin doesn't respond, his eyes grim and lifeless.

"So I assume your friend has a taste for soul food." Wil points to the video camera that's on a chair in the corner. "You just like videotaping them."

Barrick leans over to him. "Who is he?"

"He'll kill me," Martin says without a thought.

Wil nods. "He ain't the only one."

$-10-$

The car drives slowly, his hands gripped around the steering wheel, his heart hanging on for any kind of hope. David drives down the streets in his old hood and finds himself humbled and heartbroken.

The seventeenth ward will always be his home, no matter how far away he might live, no matter how far he goes in the groves of academe. These streets are the fabric of his skin and his life. These buildings and people are part of him and always will be.

And that's why it hurts even more that Kari didn't tell me about her past, he thinks. *She knows where I'm from so why couldn't she have told me where she was from?*

He parks to hand out leaflets showing a missing Mikayla, first giving them out in front of the market, then over by the barber shop and Laundromat. He asks those he sees if they've seen this little girl. The faces and voices of those he sees are empathetic, but can't help.

The more time goes by, the more helpless he's becoming.

He visits a nearby playground in the Hollygrove area just as the sun begins to start fading away.

Don't go down just yet, he thinks as he stares at the dimming light. *Don't fade on me now.*

David walks over to the familiar basketball courts and begins tacking one of the flyers to a pole. Soon he is approached by one of the players on the court, wearing baggy shorts that are almost falling down along with a whole lot of attitude.

"What's up, man?"

David ignores him and finishes the job.

"Don't be puttin' that up around here," the brother continues. "Y'all rich people think everybody from Hollygrove is criminals."

"*I'm* from Hollygrove."

The young man in his twenties looks David over, not convinced.

"Grew up right over there on Forshey near Palmetto."

The guy curses in disbelief. "I live on Forshey. Which house?"

"Baby blue one on the corner."

"You Miss Willie's son?"

David nods.

"It's me—Joey, man. I was that li'l dude who used to buy frozen cups from your momma, like almost every day!"

Joey walks up and examines the flyer that David just put up. "Is that your daughter?"

David nods.

"Damn, I'm sorry about that. . . ."

"I wanted to bring her here to see where her old man grew up. But I never got around to it after my mother died."

Joey now looks at David with concerned eyes. "Well, after you find her, you bring her by and I'll have my girl make some of her special okra gumbo."

"That's if I find her."

"They found somebody," Joey says. "'Cuz I was at City Park earlier and they had a whole SWAT team taking down some guy."

"Oh yeah?" David can't believe it. Nobody's called him. "Thanks, man. I need to check that out."

"Go take care of your business. We got you covered here, man. Gimme some of them flyers."

David gives him a pile of the flyers as he watches Joey whistle for the rest of the guys playing ball. Then the young man passes the flyers out to the guys and tells them to be on the lookout for this little girl, to let him know if they find anything, to tell others.

As David watches this, he can't help but compare these guys' reactions to his friends'.

This proves something he's just beginning to understand.

Privilege and prestige can buy you a lot of things, but it can't buy you character.

$-11-$

The words don't want to come.

Kari sits on her bed, the computer on her lap, the screen seeming to mock her. Over and over again she has tried starting the letter, but she can't.

There are too many things she wants to say and not enough words that will allow her to say them.

She's trying to take Anne's advice, writing this letter to her father. But she can't.

The dead sometimes do speak. Sometimes they mock. And in cases like this, sometimes they laugh.

She wants to tell him how strong she is, but she can't. She wants to forgive him, but she won't. She wants to tell him that he almost broke her, but she knows that's a lie.

I'm broken. Just like these fragments of sentences, I'm unfinished. Unspoken. Unworthy. Unwilling.

Soon she slams the laptop shut and lets out a curse. Then she walks over to a drawer to find the box she came across in the garage.

In front of the mirror moments later, Kari examines her mother's cross around her neck.

For a long time, she stares at the woman in front of her.

She stares and wonders.

We all carry the weight of our weary world around with us. Some just get used to their load. Some get to ignore it completely. For a few, they have help. For others, they've managed to slowly unpack their baggage over the years.

But the brokenness never fully goes away. Not in a fallen world. Not in a world full of busy people who have turned away from God and decided that they alone can carry that load.

Nobody can do it on their own.

But Lord knows we try.

Lord knows we just keep trying.

ON THE SIXTH DAY

− 1 −

E very second counts.

As Wil and Barrick look through the two-way mirror, they both know this fact.

Wil knows it too well.

"I sweated Picou all night," Barrick says in a weary voice.

The deep lines etched in her face are from things like this. Trying over and over again. Trying to no avail. Working in the dead of night *with* the dead of night. Trying and failing.

"We've got less than twenty-four hours," Wil replies.

"If this freak hasn't talked by now . . ."

"Turn off the videotape."

Barrick looks at him, knowing what he means. "That's against police procedure."

"So is killing little girls. Do it."

Barrick shakes her head and raises her eyebrows. "It's on you, Wil."

A lot will be on him if this day ends and they don't find Mikayla.

Barrick goes to turn off the recorder as Wil enters the interrogation room.

"I'm not talkin' without my lawyer," Picou says in a thick Cajun accent.

Wil nods, then sits down across from the man. He slowly places his FBI badge on the table in front of Picou, wondering if he will know what he's being shown.

"FBI. Impressive. Least now I'm talkin' to a college grad."

"See, the difference between me and Detective Barrick is that

I play by a whole other set of rules. Sometimes, I don't play by any rules."

Picou doesn't seem remotely concerned.

"Since 9/11, I can detain a suspect without due process," Wil continues. "All I gotta do is declare you a national security risk. Then it's one phone call and you're on a plane to some hellhole in the Third World."

Dark, beady, nervous eyes look over at him, yet Picou still says nothing.

"I promise: whatever your friend's gonna do to you is nothin' compared to what I got planned."

Picou swallows, but remains silent. Wil waits and watches.

"Have it your way," he says, starting to dial the cell phone.

The man interrupts his dialing. "Okay, but you gotta protect me."

"Where is he?" Wil asks.

In moments he has an address and a location. As Picou tries to demand help and assistance, Wil ignores him. When he heads to find Barrick, someone is standing next to her.

Wil realizes that David's been here watching the whole thing.

"What are you doing here?"

"I'm going with you," David says.

"No way. It's too dangerous."

"I don't give a shit! I'm coming."

For a moment, Wil tries to decide whether to make a stand here or not.

We don't have time. Every second, Wil. Every second matters.

Wil looks at the father in front of him and knows there's no way David's going to take no for an answer.

− 2 −

Wil and Barrick enter the lobby of the high-rise across from City Park, where they picked up Picou, and David follows closely behind. He obviously shouldn't be with them. But time is of the essence and they won't use it to chase him away.

"Mr. Ames, you can stay with us. But, please hang back, keep quiet. Give us the ground to do our work."

Barrick flashes a badge to the lobby clerk and asks where maintenance is located.

"Main one's in the parking garage," he man says. "The other's on the eighth floor."

"Where would we find Remy Herbert?"

"Upstairs."

In the elevator, Wil says to David. "I know you're pumped. But, stay out of the way. Follow our direction. Okay?"

When they get off the elevator, a window reveals City Park and the Carousel Gardens below. Barrick glances at him.

"Nice view, huh?" Wil says.

He doesn't expect to actually find Remy here. Not now, not today. Not since they got Picou in custody. But who knows. Stranger things have happened.

They walk steadily down the hallway. Wil notices the eerie silence and slows down, motioning with his arm for Barrick and David to do the same.

Just like that, a door opens and a skinny white man in his forties exits the room they're all headed toward.

He's right there, in front of them.

Remy sees them and bolts, heading down the hallway to a door that turns out to be stairs. He's fast like a cat.

As Barrick calls for their backup units, Wil storms into the stairwell and hears Remy's steps as he ascends to the roof. He follows with David and Barrick behind him. His mind races, but he's all action. He can't think now. All he can do is follow the lowlife to the roof with his revolver in hand and hope on his side.

For a moment he looks back at David, knowing it was a bad idea to bring him, knowing that the situation has trouble written all over it.

The door blasts open to reveal the bright sun and for a second it blinds Wil. He holds up one hand to block the rays while his other hand holds his gun. He looks and sees the figure they followed standing at the edge of the roof, looking over the railing and then back at them.

Wil holds out an arm again to tell Barrick and David to stay back.

"Go ahead, Remy—jump."

Wil doesn't take his focus off the creep.

Part of him wants to help Remy fall to his death.

Remy squints as he sucks in breaths. "Then you'll never find her."

Wil moves forward as Remy takes a step closer to the railing.

"I swear, I'll do it."

Wil keeps going. "No, you won't. You know why."

His feet keep moving closer.

Remy doesn't say anything, just looks at him and back down below.

"'Cause you're a coward. Only cowards prey on children."

Remy turns and tries to lift himself up over the steel railing, but it's too late. Wil slams against him and hears a grunt as he lands on top of the pedophile.

Wil gets off Remy, who coughs, trying to catch his breath. David suddenly pounces on the man, punching, bloodying his nose. Wil pauses a moment to let David have his way. But, just a moment.

"David, come on," Wil says, positioning himself between Remy and David. "Get back. That's enough. I got him."

The father in front of him is a man half-possessed. It takes all of Wil's strength to hold David back. Barrick is beside him helping, trying to talk sense into the father.

This is the picture of seething rage, Wil thinks as he holds back a man capable of murder at this very moment.

I'd do the same if it was my little girl.

But murder won't do them any good now. Especially not Mikayla.

— 3 —

Remy Herbert's house is spotless. The cops make note that the rooms are meticulously in order and clean. The place is an odd contrast to the man who owns it—the very picture of disorder. Perhaps the outward cleanliness counterbalances the messy shit inside of his soul.

The only thing standing out in Remy's house are the bags of candy lined up on the side of the kitchen counter as if they're ready for trick-or-treaters. But Halloween isn't even remotely close.

The candy seems to imply there's something more to Remy, but the cops continue hoping to find proof.

They go to the basement hoping for answers.

All they find is more order and cleanliness.

And nothing resembling a missing four-year-old girl.

− 4 −

David stands as he listens to the news that Detective Barrick and Wil give him. Surprisingly bittersweet news.

"We found souvenirs from the victims in Remy's van," Barrick says.

"Did any belong to Mikayla?"

"No," Wil says. "But forensics is sweeping his house as we speak."

"Then it's possible she's still alive?"

He knows that they don't like to raise parents' hopes, that they must try and be as realistic as possible. But this isn't a normal case.

"It's possible," Wil says.

Those two words are the first two of their kind since Monday came on like an attacking animal. David is weary and restless, nodding at Wil and not saying anything else. He knows he's a bloody mess, both inside and out.

He soon finds himself in the men's room washing that same weary face and glancing in the mirror. Wil walks in to use the restroom. "You talked to Kari?" Wil asks.

"She's on her way," David says. "You know, I don't think I've ever thanked you."

Wil shakes his head. "It's my job. And I'd do anything for Kari."

These words sound strange spoken by someone else.

"You love her?"

Wil finishes drying his hands and throws away the paper towel. "I've always loved her, but she's in love with you. I can see that. That's how life is—nothing fair about it. Like this case. Most parents couldn't even get the news to post their daughter's photo. They did in your case. I'm here because you could make a call to the mayor. There's a stark difference between the powerful and the powerless. You're lucky to be on the side of power."

David looks down at the dirty, tiled floor. "I don't feel powerful— and not without my family."

"At least now you know how much they mean to you. Listen, you need to ease up on Kari a little. Give her some credit for what she did. She changed her life. Your life."

"I'm trying to work my way through all of this."

Wil shoots him a cutting look. "I've seen people go through more. Don't play the victim, buddy."

David wants to take the secure, smug look of the FBI agent and flush it down the nearest toilet.

"And don't play me," David says. "I want you to stay away from my wife."

Wil nods and leaves David alone in silence.

— 5 —

Kari is heading up the stairs at the police station when she sees a face she recognizes. It's Lynette Davis. She'd looked her up online and read details about her missing child.

A group surrounds the woman, but Kari works through them to get to her. Lynette's face is pale and her cheeks are wet. Eyes that are red and lost look up at her.

"Ms. Davis. I'm Kari Ames. What's happened?"

"My baby's dead."

Kari hugs her and begins to cry. "I'm so sorry. God bless you. God bless your child."

"And you, Ms. Ames. Have they found out anything about your baby?"

Kari pulls back. "We're praying. I'll keep you in my prayers."

Kari returns to her mission and climbs up those stairs again toward her husband and the rest. She breathes out, but can't breathe back in. Once again she feels dizzy, her forehead and palms dotted with sweat.

"Lord, help me, please."

She steps into the police interrogation room to see blood covering David's shirt.

"My God! David, what happened?"

He just shakes his head. "When I saw that scum, I just lost it."

"What scum? Who?" They catch her up on what happened on the roof.

"You beat him?"

"He beat the shit out of him," Wil says as he walks up to her.

Barrick stands next to him and adds, "Problem is though, Remy Herbert didn't abduct your daughter."

Now she's shaking her head, confused and depleted, not understanding all of this.

"He just confessed to what he did," Wil continues. "Even two victims we didn't know about. The sicko said they were sacrifices he had to make to cleanse his soul."

"What about his house?" she asks.

"Went over it with a fine-tooth comb," Barrick says as she leans against a desk. "Nothing ties him to Mikayla."

She wants to crumble down on the floor, but leans against a chair.

"Turns out, six days was no coincidence—just like I thought. Even madness has its logic. And Remy Herbert had his."

David still doesn't look the slightest bit impressed. "I get it. On the sixth day, not only had God created man, but the serpent too."

"That's right," Barrick replies. "Remy had also been molested as a child. And killin' victims on the seventh day was his idea of mercy."

"That way, no one would have to live with the shame he had lived with," Wil says.

Kari looks at Wil, then looks at David. She closes her eyes for a second.

Wil seems to understand some of her thoughts. He adds, "On the good side, there's hope that Mikayla's still alive."

Hope.

And it's more than the mother downstairs has.

There's still hope for their daughter.

Still hope.

— 6 —

Words have a power to break and burn. But they also have the ability to free you, to let loose the chains that have imprisoned you for so long.

Kari sits on the edge of the bed, typing the last few words to the man she's grown accustomed to loathing. Loathing and fearing.

The words come more easily this time. She holds nothing back—no bad word, no violent wish.

"Are you all right?" David asks her.

She nods. "I'm writing a letter to my father." David looks at her curiously. "He'll never see it, but this is for me. For us. I'm trying to heal myself. So, when we find our daughter, I'll be ready to be a better mother."

— 7 —

David leaves Kari alone, thinking about another letter he wrote. A broken man writing broken words. That was all he could do. He had thought—he had hoped—that it would be enough.

The letter had been to Beth. After thinking that hiring a beautiful woman was harmless, then spending months telling himself that their relationship was harmless, David had woken up thinking he was in love with the young woman. Thinking he wanted and needed her. The physical desires mixed with the fantasy and messed with his mind.

Eventually the guilt and shame of what he was doing, along with Beth's continual want and need for more, forced him to end it.

He had written her a letter and had read it to her, knowing he needed to get the words right, yet wanting to make sure no remnants of those words were left behind.

David still remembers the letter.

Beth:

I am sorry that things have turned out like this. I am deeply sorry for failing as a man and as a Christian. I thought I could be strong enough and handle this like every other thing I've handled in my life. I didn't realize that some things were too strong for one man to deal with. Falling for you was one of those things.

These moments and this intimacy—they would be special and

precious if they belonged solely to us. But I failed my wife. I failed my baby girl. I don't know what happened except that I failed. That includes failing you.

You're an amazing woman, Beth. You deserve an amazing life. I know you've said that things could stay the same, but we both know they can't. Even if the guilt was gnawing away at me every single moment of every day, this still wouldn't be right. You deserve someone better, something more.

Forgive me, Beth. Someone so special like you is a rare thing. I realized it and soon wanted it all for myself. But we never get all we want. That's not the way life works. I know that now.

He wipes the tears in his eyes as he thinks about his indiscretions and failures once again. They will forever haunt him and David knows this now.

He wonders if God is paying him back for those sins.

He wonders if Mikayla's abduction is part of the atonement he needs to make.

He wonders if there's ever a road back from this mess he's made of his life.

Why is it so easy to fall down but so damned hard to get back up?

Why is it so easy to become broken yet so hard to put back all the pieces?

It's easy to act the part, but it's difficult to truly live with it, day in and day out.

For so long, for so many years, I've heard and sung the song, "It Is Well with My Soul." But I haven't felt that it's truly well. I haven't believed that it could ever be well.

But God gives us a day of rest every week, and with this rest comes glimmers of hope.

Hope for our baby girl.

And hope for her momma. A broken woman who needs to truly believe it can be well with her soul.

Maybe it finally will be.

ON THE SEVENTH DAY

— 1 —

Kari dreams of sunrise on Lake Pontchartrain. In her dream, she's a hummingbird, floating and flying and watching her reflection below on the still water.

Not another soul is around. There is a stillness that gives her joy. More than that, the stillness gives her peace.

The sun is a reminder that God hasn't forgotten us. That God is still in charge. That the same sun He created so long ago is still there, still bright and blazing and still rising just like His glory.

Kari flies and she hears a humming noise. Not of her wings but rather of some sweet, old-time gospel song. She doesn't know it by heart, yet it still seems so familiar, so perfect.

She wonders if this is Heaven, yet she knows that others await in Heaven.

Does my baby girl?

She continues flying as the sun continues rising.

It's a new day. And that hope is rising within her. Little by little.

– 2 –

Wil had woken this morning with an idea. Not just an idea, but an idea to act upon. He'd called Detective Barrick first thing to make sure they could get moving right away. After taking a quick shower and ignoring breakfast, he was headed down to the police station.

The workaholic Barrick greeted him as he walked in. Now they were heading over to talk with Frank, the CSI officer.

"This is Special Agent Bennett," Barrick says to Frank, who's casually sipping a cup of coffee.

"I want another look at M. K.'s boot prints," Wil says without further chitchat.

Frank nods. "Suit yourself."

The beanpole of a man slowly opens the filing cabinet that's in his desk. Then he carefully looks to see which file it is. It appears that there are maybe a hundred files his fingers are scanning through. As he does, Wil shoots Barrick a look that says, *Let's get this over with.*

Frank finally opens a file and yanks out a picture. "These are the prints found at the Ames house and the nearby levee."

Wil nods, eager to see more.

"Those are from the other victims," Frank says giving him more photos.

It takes Wil a few moments to compare the photos. He points a finger at the photo from the Ames house. "Can you magnify that?"

Frank is taking another sip of coffee. "Yeah, on the computer, but—"

"Just do it."

Barrick looks a little surprised at the authority in Wil's voice, but she gets it. She seems to understand his urgency, especially considering the fact that they found M. K. and he didn't have Mikayla.

It takes a few moments as Frank gets the picture up on his computer and then magnifies the photo.

"There you go," Frank says, moving away from the screen. "That's four hundred percent magnification."

"Keep going."

The boot print on the screen continues to be enlarged.

"There—stop."

Wil looks over Frank's shoulder and then turns around toward Barrick.

"Look, wear and tear's different than the prints from the other abductions. These boots have been worn for some time. It also appears that Remy Herbert favors his right leg."

Frank now sees what he's saying. He gives Wil a look that seems surprised and impressed.

"Maybe the perp bought new boots," Barrick suggests.

"Only the depth of the imprint found at the Ames home is considerably shallower."

Barrick shakes her head, her eyes going back and forth from Wil to the computer screen. "Not sure I follow."

Frank turns around in his chair. "The depth of the imprint is inconsistent with Remy's weight. Of course, there is also the soil composition to factor in."

Barrick and Wil continue looking at the photos on the screen.

"Unless this pedophile's tiptoeing through the tulips," Frank adds.

"The press did leak details about his MO," Wil says. This is what he was thinking when he woke up. "My guess is that whoever made these prints had to wear a couple of pairs of socks to fit into the boot size worn by M. K. Which means . . . we're dealing with a copycat. Let's get everyone in here who ever had anything to do with this kid."

— 3 —

In the next few hours, Wil and Barrick interview everyone they can with a connection to the Ameses—from their jobs, from church, friends, and relatives. Soon they find themselves talking to Tia at her mansion, the last place she saw or spoke to Kari.

"How is she doing?" Tia asks about Kari.

This surprises Wil. "She's managing. So you're one of her closest friends?"

Tia nods, wipes a tear in her eye. "I haven't been much of a friend this week."

"And why's that?" Barrick asks.

"Just everything happening, with her past coming out. A lot of people think Kari has something to do with Mikayla's disappearance."

"Do you?"

"No," Tia tells the detective. "Absolutely not. She loves that girl more than life itself. She'd do anything for her."

"You never had any questions about your friend's past history?"

"No. I know she had family issues, but don't we all? The fact that I never met her parents doesn't mean anything. I met her when she was already with David. They're the perfect couple. Well, that's what it seemed anyway."

"Have you seen any problems between the Ameses?" Wil asks.

"No. None. I know Kari went through a bout of depression after Mikayla was born, but that wasn't anything. David's been a wonderful husband."

"Did you ever take care of Mikayla?"

"I watched Mikayla for Kari all the time, but when I wasn't available—which was rare—she would call Beth," Tia says.

"Beth Hutchins, who is Mr. Ames's assistant?"

"Yes. Have you spoken to her?" Tia asks the officers.

"Not yet. Do you think we should?"

"Yes. Why not?

"What kind of person is Beth?" Barrick asks.

"Well, she's good-looking, but I don't know her very well and . . ." She hesitates. "I never cared too much for her."

This surprises Wil and he looks up at her from his notes.

"I don't think her behavior is always . . . appropriate."

"What do you mean?"

"She's flirty."

"Are you Beth?" Wil asks out of courtesy.

"That's me. Can I help you?"

Wil introduces himself as Barrick shows her badge and does the same.

"We need to ask you a few questions in relationship to the Ames case."

"I already told the police everything I know," she says in a calm, polite way.

"We're just rechecking some facts," Wil asks. "How many students does Professor Ames fail in a term?"

"About eight percent," Beth says without thinking.

"Do you think any of them hold a grudge against David?" Barrick asks.

"They're not happy, that's for sure."

"Unhappy enough to take his little girl?"

Beth shakes her head. "That's a big accusation. You think someone would do that just because of a bad grade?"

"Maybe it's about more than a bad grade. We're looking at all the possibilities," the detective states. "Does anyone who has a beef with the professor come to mind? Anyone at all?"

Beth thinks, but then shakes her head again. "Sorry I can't be more helpful."

"I understand you babysat for the Ameses on occasion. You must be close to the family. Was that part of your job as assistant to Mr. Ames, or were you paid separately?" he asks.

She nods, again looking unfazed by the line of questioning. "I volunteered, though they paid me later. A girl has to do what she has to do. Especially when putting herself through college. I'm just glad I could help out. I love being around David's little girl. She looks up to me. Plus, it was good for the Ameses to have a night out. Especially with David's busy schedule."

"Are you married, Ms. Hutchins?"

"No, not yet."

Her eyebrows and lips both rise at the same time, adding a nice, suggestive exclamation point to their discussion.

— 4 —

Attractive girl," Barrick tells Wil back outside as they're headed toward his car.

"Yeah. Maybe too attractive."

"What's that supposed to mean?" Barrick fires back.

"I just got a feeling."

"And why's that? Just because a young woman is attractive means she might know something more?"

Wil nods and understands the detective's defensiveness. "It's not Beth I got the feeling about. It's David. A man might be happily married and not think for a second he'd be interested in another woman, but it doesn't mean that the thought doesn't still cross your mind. Any man—*any* man—would think twice when it came to Beth."

"Maybe the professor is different."

"Yeah, maybe."

— 5 —

Too often in life, we neglect to do the hard yet necessary things until it's too late.

Yet for Kari, this is one time when it's not going to be too late. At least as far as this is concerned.

It took a while to drive here, and all throughout that drive she wondered if she should be doing this. There were other things to be done, other problems to deal with. Yet here she was now, walking through this graveyard that she hadn't set foot in for years, kneeling by the headstone she once vowed never to see again.

It's not too late to let go.

Kari glances down at the name.

Nelson Carter.

Kari reaches in her purse and removes the letter. She places it against the headstone, looking down at it for a moment.

She stays there for a while, staring at the headstone, knowing she'll never truly forget the past, but also knowing it doesn't have to weigh her down the rest of her life.

— 6 —

When Wil pulls up to the Ames house, he finds the garage door open. For a minute he thinks it might be Kari—hopes it might be her. But it's David clearing out a section of the garage. Wil greets him and notices that the boxes are full of old records.

"What's all this?" Wil asks. "Moving out?"

"You wish," David answers. "No, we're gonna use some of these old boxes to put Mikayla's flyers in. I'm bringing them inside."

David picks up two boxes. Another remains by his feet.

"Let me help you," Wil says.

He picks up the box and follows David into the house. They head to the library, which looks even messier than when Wil last saw it.

"We've talked to everyone from Kari's past," Wil says as they walk. "Nothing ties back to her."

"Well, that's a relief."

They set the boxes next to others on the floor. David doesn't particularly appear to be in the mood for entertaining or chatting, so Wil gets down to business.

"With Remy no longer a suspect, we're grasping at straws here."

David nods, looking at one of the windows, lost in his thoughts. Wil moves closer to him.

"I know we've gone over some of this before, but I'd like to ask you a few more questions if you don't mind."

"Ask away."

"How many students would you estimate you've taught at Tulane?"

David shrugs. "Thousands."

"And you still think not one of them went sideways? Kinda defies the odds of probability."

"The occasional student gets upset about a grade," David replies. "But I talk to them about it. If there were any problems beyond that, Beth would know."

"How is your relationship to Beth? What kind of person is she?"

"She's an excellent worker. Bright and intelligent. Great with the students. Very articulate."

"I know," Wil says. "I spoke to her."

David raises his eyebrows. "So what'd she say?"

"Same thing as you."

David doesn't say anything more.

"Ever had a *thing* with a student?" he asks the professor.

David's head jerks and his eyes grow wider. "You mean an affair?"

He looks at Wil carefully, then adds, "No."

"How about with one of your TAs?"

David's nose wrinkles with disgust. "Get the hell out of my house!"

Wil closely watches David. But he leaves without saying anything more.

− 7 −

Sometimes Wil likes to go off on his own and find someplace he's never been, to think. To get up and out of the routine and think about everything. So, he drives down a strange side street in New Orleans, the sun beating down on him. He parks to eat a hot dog he's bought and finally decides to make a call.

"Ames isn't telling us everything," Wil tells Barrick. "Something is up with him and that Beth chick. I get the feeling she's holding out too. They get real touchy when asked about each other."

"Well, since we've given so much time to outing the missus, we may as well dig a little deeper about the churchgoing college professor. Maybe he's got some skeletons in a closet."

— 8 —

The sanctuary is empty and covered in shadows. Kari goes to the front and kneels on the floor before the altar. This place is familiar, but she's never seen it like this. Not because of silence and darkness but because of her silent, dark soul.

She prays like she's never prayed before.

"Dearest Heavenly Father, please reach down and touch this poor sinner. Wrap Your hands around my soul and lift it gently. Lift me up, Lord. Lift me a little bit."

She comes before her Heavenly Father like a newborn, begging to be given fresh breath and fresh life.

"I know You control everything and You hear our prayers. Lord, please hear mine. Hear my words. Please, Lord. Please."

She wipes away the tears on her cheeks.

"I know they say that God is love and I need a little of that love, Lord. I need just a teardrop to fall down on me. I need some grace and mercy, but most of all I need some love. Love to fill my caved-in heart and love to share with others. I need Your love, Lord."

Kari prays out loud and doesn't hear the steps of the person who comes in and stands behind her.

"True faith is believing when it's hardest to believe, Lord," she says. "I just couldn't see Your plan. I'm still not sure I see it. But I'm gonna believe anyway. I have to believe. No matter what happens, because you've never let me down. Just promise, Lord, You'll watch over my baby."

Behind her, watching over Kari, is the quiet figure of Bishop Jakes.

"If you're a forgiving God, then I need you to forgive me, because I've finally forgiven myself."

Kari's cries continue to be heard as the bishop silently leaves without ever telling her he was there.

− 9 −

She can hear the voice of Bishop Jakes and one of his last messages filling her heart.

We live in a world where we have to grasp and claw our way to get ahead. Or perhaps simply just get by.

Kari is no longer waiting but acting. She's finally beginning to start over again.

We live in a world where we try to do it ourselves in our own way. With our own timing for our own journey. We believe in the destination, but want to control the journey.

She knows the bishop is right.

We fight so hard to keep holding on to things. Stupid, foolish things. We hold on so tight and never let go.

Kari has been holding on for some time. For a long time.

We hold on before Someone finally gives us the courage to let go!

And on this seventh day, this day of rest, Kari is finding peace about letting go.

Peace comes in collecting every drop of alcohol in the house and shoving it into a dark trash bag.

Peace comes in dumping that trash bag in a trash can out in the garage.

Peace comes in ripping off all the information about M. K. off the wall and putting it in another trash bag along with notes and print-outs and maps and papers.

Peace comes in accepting that we can't do it all and that we have to let go.

As the old saying goes: let go and let God.

−10−

David sits in the familiar chair in his office at the university, wondering what to do and who to talk to. Suddenly his world feels like an isolated jail cell.

The little reminders and the thoughts and feelings—they keep blossoming and getting bigger.

He's tried to block out the questions and the doubts for a whole week, but he can't any longer. He's tired. But more than that, David is heavy with guilt and regret.

He's fought off wondering if Beth has anything to do with Mikayla's disappearance. He still thinks there's no way, that it's just another part of his secret story, a story that doesn't have to come up right now.

Yet he suddenly has doubts. About everything.

He picks up the phone and dials a number. But Beth's answering service picks up. He doesn't leave a message.

He knows he needs to see her in person.

—11—

Wil doesn't know what to expect this time when he knocks on this door. But he's relieved to see the beautiful, smiling face.

"I was just thinking of you," Kari tells him. "Come on in."

It's close to evening and the light outside is beginning to fade. They go to the library, where Wil sees a large pile of flyers for Mikayla alongside some of the boxes David used for storing records.

"More flyers, huh?"

Kari nods. "I printed out another thousand to send to search groups in Plaquemines Parish."

He nods, unsure how to tell her the news. "The bureau wants me back in Baton Rouge."

She doesn't look surprised. "Guess you gotta go home sometime."

Kari continues taking the records out of the boxes, being careful with them.

"That's all you're gonna say?"

She stops and looks up at him. "What do you want me to say?"

"If I have to tell you, then nothing."

"Wil, I know you love me, in a way no one ever has. Even if I never gave you a whole lot in return."

"We have a second chance, Kari. How many people get that in life?"

"This isn't a second chance," Kari says. "Just because my marriage and my life are in shambles doesn't mean I get to simply start over again. That's not how it works. That's not how it should work."

"I'm just saying—"

"I know what you're saying. And I'm saying that I love David.

Marriage is about working hard. About forgiving. About dealing with someone else through the storms of life. Like this one."

"You think it's an accident that I'm here?" Wil says. "That after all this time, we still have feelings for each other."

"You're a big FBI agent and wearing those rose-colored glasses?" She puts her hands on her hips.

Wil only smiles.

"God didn't bring me this far," Kari says. "He didn't bring David and me this far to give up on each other and our child. I don't know what's gonna happen and don't need to know anything except that my baby is coming home, and in one piece."

Her eyes move off him and onto the floor. Wil waits, but doesn't get anything from her. He looks and sees a picture of the Ames family on the wall. The reminder hurts just like Kari's silence.

"Come on," she finally says, giving him a pat on the arm—a friendly, brotherly pat. "Help me empty these boxes before I start crying again. And I *know* you don't want that."

Wil nods and then puts his gun on the nearby desk, rolling up his sleeve to help her.

"Where should I start?"

Kari points at a box. "How about that one over there?"

They're at it for ten minutes until something stops Kari.

She lets what's in her hand fall to the floor. He walks over and picks it up.

A photo of Beth, wearing lingerie.

"Well now," he says, a lightbulb turning on again in his mind and a pain for Kari running through his heart.

He looks back at Kari and knows that expression. He turns the photo over and places it on the desk just as Kari begins to start opening more albums. He remains quiet, but begins to do the same.

"He does this," she says slowly and carefully, almost through clenched teeth. "Then he judges me?"

Over the next few moments, they discover more things from

Beth, including several cards and a letter. Kari reads every one of them, each word, and with every passing moment appears blinded with surprise and shock.

"David picked her up from the abortion clinic," she tells Wil as she sits on the couch. "She talked about the grief of losing their child."

Wil doesn't say what he's thinking.

Kari just looks at him. Wil can feel his heart racing. He knows what's happened now. What's happened, and what they must do.

Kari puts her hands to her head. "No," she says, without saying the rest of what is running through her mind.

"I've got to call the station," Wil says, excusing himself to the kitchen.

He's on the phone as Kari walks in behind him. She hears, "Yes, *Beth Hutchins,*" he says again slowly. "David's TA."

Barrick barks back at him on the phone and that's when he hears the door shut.

He looks around the front and sees Kari, now approaching the driveway.

Wil thinks of David trying to beat Remy Herbert to a pulp. Then he thinks of Kari and knows that she's capable of doing the same.

He curses as he tears out the front door and sees Kari in her Lexus starting to drive off.

"Kari, what're you doing?" he shouts.

But the mother and her car are screeching away, gone.

Wil goes into the library, remembering his gun. It's not where he left it.

He knows it's in Kari's hands now.

God knows what she's about to do with it.

−12−

She has never taken this long to reach anyplace. The last thing Kari wants is to get pulled over for speeding and for a cop to see the gun that's on the passenger's seat. Rage fills her.

It didn't seem long ago that she let go of the anger and fear directed toward her father. But now, there's a new tsunami of fury unleashing in her soul, directed at this long-legged tramp who somehow managed to steal both her husband and her daughter. But more than that, the rage is directed toward David.

A million thoughts ride with her and every one blames him.

She can't shake them off or drive faster than them. Instead, she lets them fuel her anger.

Every time she blinks she can only see Mikayla.

Poor Mikayla, Kari thinks.

Suffering from the sins of her mother and her father.

Suffering for no reason other than that.

By the time Kari pulls up close to the address she punched into her GPS, the outside light is gone and darkness is draped over the neighborhood.

But the seventh day isn't done yet and neither is Kari.

−13−

First she pounds on the front door, but nobody answers.

Kari's imagination goes crazy. Beth could be gone. Could have left town. Beth *and* David could be gone and taken Mikayla.

She bangs on the door again and waits.

With the gun in her hand, Kari heads toward a closed window and looks in. The drapes are pulled, but there are lights on. A car is in the driveway.

She begins to head around to the back of the house.

$-14-$

Wil is speeding through New Orleans yelling at Barrick, who's on the phone. It takes him a few moments to tell the detective what's happened.

"She's en route to Beth Hutchins. And she's got my gun."

"We're on our way," Barrick tells him.

It all ends like this. Tonight. At this house.

Wil can't get there quick enough.

When the back door refuses to budge, Kari uses the butt of the gun to break a window. She clears the frame of some broken glass and climbs through, cutting her arms and legs. She doesn't even pause to see that she's already injured herself.

She races through the home, finding a family-room mantle lit with candles. As she examines it more closely, she sees that it is almost like an altar with a photo in the center of the candles.

It's a sonogram. A picture of Beth's lost baby.

It makes her both sad and sick at the same time.

Just as Kari is about to turn, she hears the shuffling of steps coming from behind her.

"What are you doing in my house?" Beth demands.

"Where is she? Where's my daughter?"

Kari almost startles herself with the sound of her voice. She holds the gun steady, hoping that Beth doesn't see the trembling that's racing through her entire body.

Beth is wearing a silk robe and shakes her head with mock confusion. "I don't know what you're talking about."

"Stop bullshitting, Beth! Bring me my baby!"

Kari looks around for any signs of Mikayla. In the corner of the room sits a pair of Blundstone boots.

"You either tell me where Mikayla is right now or—"

"Or what? What you gonna do? Kill me?"

The voice speaking to her is a taunt from her past, a joke from the streets. It's the same damned thing. The same voice telling her she's weak and no good and worthless and silly.

"You're nothing but a damn housewife. And you ain't so good at the wife part either. That's why your man came running to me. Least I knew how to satisfy him."

Everything in her wants to press the trigger.

"Where is she?" Kari demands.

"The whole world doesn't revolve just around you, Kari Ames, trying to be Ms. Perfect."

"You have no idea."

Beth gives her a mocking smile. "I have a pretty good idea."

Kari's not about to sit around and talk and argue with this woman.

"Mikayla!" She points the gun at Beth and forces her to sit on the couch. "You stay right there or I will hurt you."

And then Kari hears something, faint and weak, but there— actually there.

Kari looks all around, up and down, to her left and right. She knows the voice is real this time, but isn't sure where it's coming from.

"Baby! Where are you?"

Beth keeps looking at her and the gun.

"Down here, Mommy!"

Then suddenly Beth begins to run toward her as she says, "I won't let you take her!"

Kari shoves Beth backward, against a small table holding a vase with an orchid. All of them crash to the wood floor. Kari ignores them and then finds the door where the voice came from.

The basement.

The dark, dank basement.

She rushes down the steps, continuing to hear Mikayla's voice. She calls out her name and finally confirms that it's her daughter that she hears screaming behind a storage closet door.

"Lemme out! Mommy! Please, Mommy!"

Tears are in her eyes and she pounds on the locked handle with her fist and then the gun. Soon the wood breaks and separates and she's able to yank the door open.

The figure inside the dark is a tiny, little girl. But it's her baby girl. And she's alive and breathing and crying and wrapping her arms around her mommy.

"Dear God, thank you, dear God." Kari cries into the darkness, holding on to her child.

"It's okay, baby. Mommy's here. Everything's okay."

She looks down at Mikayla's face. Angelic, startling in its beauty, so wonderful. Kari wipes the tears off her daughter's face.

Then, suddenly, Mikayla's smile turns to horror as she looks at something behind her mommy.

Something strikes Kari's arm just as she has time to see it coming out of nowhere. The pain is hot and intense and forces her to drop the gun. Kari shields Mikayla and herself and sees Beth holding a long fireplace iron like the demon that she is.

Kari shoves her back and then lunges out toward the woman, gripping her by the neck. She manages to push Beth back against the wall of the basement.

Out of breath, still holding the fireplace iron, Beth says, "David needs to know what it feels like to lose a child!"

Beth attacks, swinging the iron. Kari dodges the first couple of blows, but one lands on her shoulder.

"Mikayla, run!" she shouts out.

Mikayla sprints to the stairs and an enraged, out-of-her-mind Beth follows. Mikayla stumbles a bit, allowing Beth to raise the long iron over her head.

Kari lunges for the gun on the floor and picks it up, then fires it, hitting the figure attacking her daughter squarely in the back.

Mikayla is on the ground, crouching in terror and screaming, just as Beth drops the iron and crumbles to the floor.

Kari rushes over to the scene and stands above the bleeding, grimacing figure on the floor. She stares down and aims the gun, knowing that she has every right and every reason to shoot.

Kari cocks the trigger as the woman beneath her pleads and screams and begs for her life. But Kari doesn't hear anything now.

And then . . .

The sweet, innocent eyes of Mikayla look up at her.

Kari remembers eyes like that. Ones that looked at a father with fear. Ones that looked at a pimp with anger. Ones that looked in a mirror with regret.

She sighs and then looks down at Beth.

She lowers the gun as she steps over Beth. "You're not worth it," Kari says as she goes over and scoops Mikayla in her arms.

—16—

Depleted and tormented, David pulls up to Beth's house.

There's a reason he's here. He's here for one reason, but the sight of his family Lexus changes that.

"What is she doing here?" he says, knowing his wife must be the driver.

He doesn't realize that he's left the car running or the door opened when he rushes toward the front door. It's locked, but he finds the spare key under a flowerpot nearby. The door opens, but he doesn't find anybody inside.

"Kari? Beth?"

The voice seems to disappear and he doesn't hear or see anybody.

"Kari—where are you?"

"Down here!"

David rushes toward the open basement door and then descends the stairs.

He sees Kari's face first, flushed and tired and teary-eyed. Then he sees Mikayla.

Nearby is the body of Beth, writhing in pain.

David rushes to his daughter's side and wraps his arms around her and Kari, who is still holding her. "Thank God," David says. "Thank you, Father."

The sweet sound of the heavens and the angels open up with one glorious word by Mikayla: "Daddy!"

−17−

Soon the house is full of cops and paramedics and detectives and others swarming around the scene. Kari watches as Beth is placed on a gurney and taken out of the basement and into an ambulance. David holds Mikayla without any sign of letting go while Kari is questioned by the detective.

Everything feels like it's traveling at a hundred miles an hour. Every thought and every breath. She wants to scoop up Mikayla and take her out of here and then just leave. Yet she knows she has to stay here, that she has things she needs to do.

David gives her an ashamed look. Kari doesn't look away.

She understands that look on his face.

We're all sinners before our Maker, she thinks.

Wil is nearby in the family room talking to Barrick when Kari leans over to Mikayla and tells her, "I'll be right back."

She looks up at David to make sure he heard her, then she goes over to talk to Wil. Barrick goes to talk to the other cops in the house.

"Mikayla okay?" Wil asks.

She nods. "She's a survivor. Just like her momma."

"Look, I . . . ," she begins to say to him.

"You don't have to say anything," Wil says gently, touching her arm. "Like I said, my eyes were wide open."

Kari glances into the tender eyes of the man who once loved her and still loves her and probably always will. Then she glances at her husband, who she loves and knows isn't as perfect as he might have seemed. He has a lot of explaining to do. He needs to fill in a lot of blanks. But they've gone through enough and both of them need to be there for Mikayla. And for each other.

She swallows and forces a smile for Wil. "Thank you. For everything."

As Wil leaves the house, Kari moves over to be by Mikayla. She takes her daughter in her arms.

"Who was that, Mommy?"

Kari looks down at Mikayla. "Best friend I ever had."

–18–

David hears footsteps coming down the stairs. He's been waiting in the living room for some time, wondering if Kari would even come down.

"She's finally asleep," she says as she enters the room.

He nods, grateful that Mikayla is finally with them again and that she's managed to fall asleep.

He's also grateful that Kari is down here standing across from him. He sighs. "I'm sorry."

"You should be," Kari says. "Talk to me, David. Let's both just talk."

She sits next to him, but leaves a distance.

"I let down my guard," David admits. "It didn't just happen. It was gradual. I thought—I truly believed—I could be strong."

"But why?" Kari asks.

"I've asked myself that. For a while—after Mikayla was born—everything seemed too overwhelming. My job and the new child and your depression. The fact that our relationship suddenly changed. And I'm not blaming anyone or anything—I did it. It was my mistake. I'm the one responsible for this mess."

"But I was at fault too," she adds. Kari sighs. "Our problems started before Mikayla was kidnapped. I kept a part of myself hidden from you. We weren't honest with each other."

David's face looks hurt and humbled. "So many times, I wanted to say something."

"But you didn't."

"I didn't want to lose you."

Kari thinks about it and nods. "I guess we were in the same boat."

"I love you, Kari."

She seems to study his face, wondering who he is and what's going on inside of him.

"I love you too, David."

She pauses and continues looking at him with that beautiful, deep, haunting look of hers. "Maybe we'll find forgiveness for each other in that."

"Let's go back upstairs and stay close to our baby," Kari says.

When both of his girls are asleep, David heads outside to the porch and sits on the rocking chair. A clear sky is lit by a swelling full moon. The last time he sat here, he thought he'd lost both Kari and Mikayla. He'd sat here begging and pleading with God above to give him one more chance, to give him one more break, promising Him that he would change and be a better husband and father.

The glow of the moon stares back at him. He thanks God for answering his prayers and for giving him grace.

That night, as I held my baby girl in my arms, I didn't know if I was dreaming or awake. I couldn't believe I'd almost lost her, that we'd almost lost our sweet Mikayla. As she slept by my side, her breathing so steady and so strong, I wondered what I'd have done if I'd lost her.

Then I was reminded once again.

God lost His son once.

He allowed Him to come down and die for sinners like David and me.

I shivered at this thought, knowing I couldn't do the same. Knowing I wasn't that strong, that loving, that . . .

Knowing that as hard as I tried, I still wasn't God.

He was the only one who could handle today and tomorrow and the next.

God was the only one willing to stand by me and love me and hold me.

God was the only one always there.

I still had so long to go, but I knew that someone would always be holding me as I went.

SEVEN WEEKS LATER

— 1 —

"Like most of you, I was molested," Kari says before a room of thirty women. Anne had called to congratulate her on finding her child and to invite her back to a meeting. "I was twelve when my own father touched me. My dad missed my momma so much, he tried to make me her."

Voices in the audience echoed, "Take your time, take your time."

"After that, I just started to rebel. I hung out a lot, skipped school, and before long I was trying to hide my pain with drugs. Then you know the rest—when the drugs got to be too expensive, I started hookin' to pay for my habit."

Anne is smiling like a happy, proud mother.

"Anne was so good to me, she tried to help me, but I ran away. And then, I created a new world—or at least what I thought was a new world and a new me."

David is with her, standing in the back of the room. It hurts him to hear her talking about these terrible things, but he is proud of her.

"When my child got taken away from me, my entire universe exploded. Everyone found out who I really was—my husband detested me, my so-called friends threw me away. Every morning it was hard to open my eyes. I started to drink again. I couldn't take the thought of my baby being taken by a child molester. I relapsed into darkness. That's why I came back here. It was about getting well so I could find my daughter. A good friend reminded me never to be ashamed to ask for help!"

Kari looks out at the group, hoping her words might help someone else, that her story might help their story.

"Thanks for having me," she finally says.

When she looks at David, she realizes she hasn't seen him smile at her so sweetly in a long, long time.

— 2 —

In the middle of Mikayla's birthday party, the doorbell rings. It's been a smaller affair with just a couple of friends over: Wayne and Pam are here along with David and Kari's new friends Joey and Cindy, who are from Hollygrove. Mikayla still seems to be the same energetic and excited little girl who's just turned five. Kari and David continue to thank God throughout the day that they can celebrate this milestone.

Kari answers the door and is surprised to find Tia standing there, holding a wrapped present in her hands.

"Don't slam the door," Tia says.

It's been weeks since she's talked to her friend. "I'm not gonna slam the door, Tia."

"Will you ever forgive me for letting you down?"

"Girl—that's already done. Come here."

Kari hugs Tia and can't help getting teary-eyed.

It seems that every day brings the opportunity to find grace and forgiveness.

"Where's Les?" Kari eventually asks.

"I dumped that garbage in the trash, where he belonged. We've been separated for three weeks now. I plan on getting a divorce."

Kari hugs Tia again, not glad to hear the news no matter how good it might seem to be. They eventually go into the living room, where Tia greets everyone.

"Hello, David," she says as she hugs him. "I like your new look."

David grins and rubs his beard. "I thought it was time for me to look a little more scholarly."

Tia has arrived just in time for the birthday cake. It wasn't long ago that Kari had lit a candle on a cake and brought it into this room. Yet this time, there's someone to blow out the candle.

She's beautiful and bold and at five already knows a little about how dark the world can be. Yet at five, Mikayla also can forget pretty easily. As they sing "Happy Birthday" to her, Mikayla beams and then makes a wish.

As she does, Kari makes a wish too.

Lord, I pray that You give Mikayla a long and happy life. And I pray that one day she will know and love You the way You love her.

Mikayla blows out the candle and everybody claps.

Once again, Kari finds tears coming to her eyes.

These days, it's easy to appreciate every single thing. Big or small.

David holds Mikayla's hand as they walk into the crowded Higher Ground Church. They're walking behind Joey and his family. He spots his country-club friends in their usual section of the pews, the section he'd normally be heading to. But today, he decides to pick two seats next to a familiar-faced woman whom he'd seen the Sunday before it all happened.

"These seats taken?" he asks.

"All yours," the gaunt, hard face says.

David and Mikayla sit down. For a moment, David knows that exteriors can be deceiving. Who knows what kind of light shines deep inside the woman next to him?

Soon Bishop Jakes takes the podium to greet everybody.

"Good morning!" an enthusiastic and energized voice calls out.

"Good morning!" the congregation responds.

"Gotta lot on my mind, so watch out!" Bishop Jakes says.

Several parishioners reply with an "Amen!"

"Today, I wanna talk about penance," the Bishop begins. "Sounds serious, don't it? *Penance.* Whenever I hear that word, I think: folks better get outta God's way!"

David can hear several chuckles around him.

"But it's just another way of saying that you regret what you've done. There's nothing stronger than a person on the comeback!"

David listens and is moved by the words of Bishop Jakes. They are more than just a jolt of caffeine being sipped at his table in the morning. They are fuel and fire and they break away the fearful parts still clinging inside of him.

"There is a Savior ready to pick you up, bind your wounds, restore you, and move you higher than you've ever been before."

The father grips the hand of his daughter as the Spirit continues to move inside of his heart. Soon the choir begins to sing, "We Fall Down."

But we get up, David hears and reminds himself. *But we get up.*

— 4 —

Kari sings a new song in the choir.

"It's not too late," the song goes.

And as she does, she sees the smiling face of Mikayla waving at her. Kari sings and smiles and waves back.

"For a saint is just a sinner who fell down and got up."

She sees David standing next to Mikayla.

Kari's smiles, knowing they're all together in God's house. She hopes and prays that they'll be together for a long, blessed time.

It was fitting that Mikayla was found on the seventh day. Like the seven colors of the rainbow. Or the seven notes on a musical scale.

God has always placed an importance on numbers and this was no different.

The darkness I'd felt during those seven days had always been full of hope, but I'd never felt it.

God had never failed. Even if it looked that way at times.

But today, on this seventh day that God had given us, the Ames family would finally rest.

ACKNOWLEDGMENTS

There are a number of people who contributed in countless ways to my experience in writing this book.

My gratitude to my wife, Serita, and my entire family, who generously shared me with this manuscript. I will always appreciate your love and support. I also want to acknowledge the compassion and encouragement that I constantly received from my church family, The Potter's House of Dallas.

Thank you, Jan Miller, my literary agent, and a special thanks to Travis Thrasher for your prolific literary experience and ability to enhance my ideas.

Thank you to everyone at Atria, my publisher, Judith Curr, and my editor, Malaika Adero. You all treated me and my work with great dignity and integrity.